Robert Ludlow Fowler

Codification in the State of New York

Second Edition

Robert Ludlow Fowler

Codification in the State of New York
Second Edition

ISBN/EAN: 9783337418793

Printed in Europe, USA, Canada, Australia, Japan

Cover: Foto ©Andreas Hilbeck / pixelio.de

More available books at **www.hansebooks.com**

CODIFICATION

IN

THE STATE OF NEW YORK.

BY

ROBT. LUDLOW FOWLER.

SECOND EDITION, WITH ADDENDA.

New York :
MARTIN B. BROWN, PRINTER AND STATIONER,
NOS. 49 AND 51 PARK PLACE.
1884.

INTRODUCTION TO SECOND EDITION.

At the request of several friends of Mr. Field's Code I have consented to a reprint of my answers to Mr. Carter's general objections to codification. The opportunity has enabled me to amend the text of the original in several particulars which further reflection dictated, and to add important authorities. The alterations are not extensive; in the reprint, as in the original, no more has been attempted than to present the answers usually made to such objections to codification as those so forcibly re-stated by Mr. Carter in "The Proposed Codification of the Common Law." In the only two instances where Mr. Carter has seen fit to make specific objections to the "Civil Code," reported by Mr. Field, there I have endeavored to outline the argument on the other side of the question, but there my undertaking ended ; more than this would have been unwarranted in a publication which professed to be only an answer, not a treatise.

R. L. F.

New York, *November* 1, 1884.

In a letter of the date of January 29th last, Mr. Field requested me to undertake the preparation of an answer to Mr. James C. Carter's paper against codification, but the time allotted was much too brief for my opportunities. Since then Mr. Field has published his " Short Response," which has rendered any further answer unnecessary. Notwithstanding this, when Mr. Field learned that I had made some progress in the direction indicated, he politely urged me to complete and publish what I had begun. I have accordingly done so, although fully realizing that he will be disappointed with the little I have been able to add to the discussion concerning a greatly needed reform.

R. L. F.

NEW YORK, May 1, 1884.

CODIFICATION

STATE OF NEW YORK.

The Philosophic historians regard civilization as the product of certain forces, chief among which is an unceasing struggle after truth. For truth, men contend to an almost inconceivable extent, and, in the main, conscientiously; thus it is that they become unwitting factors in an accumulating civilization. The recognition of this fact will serve to disembarrass the controversy concerning the Civil Code of New York from that atmosphere of refined denigration of men and measures into which it has unfortunately fallen :

" Sed facilis cuivis rigidi censura cachinni."

In any fair discussion of a great public question it is necessary to assume, in the absence of proof, that the disputants upon either side are animated only by the most elevated motives, or else truth will, in the side issue, inevitably elude pursuit. In New York this first canon of parliamentary debate has not always been borne in mind, and the result has not been favorable to the merits of the discussion concerning the Code—a discussion which in reality relates to one of the greatest problems of the time : Shall the form of the law be more simple ?

Codification is not rightly understood without some reference to the larger subject, Jurisprudence. Jurisprudence, towering as it does, over the cognate social sciences, political economy and ethics, or deontology, has always attracted to itself a good share of the higher mental effort. The result of repeated investigations in the direction of the elements of jurisprudence has been the discovery of certain truths which are universally conceded, and in the place of which no person familiar with the jural sciences now feels at liberty to substitute conflicting hypotheses. So true is this, that any speculation, however captivating, which disregards the accumulated knowledge of the modern scientific jurists, stands as little chance of taking a permanent place in the opinions of men as would a treatise on the solar system which ignores the discoveries of a Kepler or a Laplace. Another result of the labors of the scientific jurists has been a highly developed terminology with its verbal signs for complex ideas : without recourse to this received terminology, the most accurate reasoner on jurisprudence must become, at times, inexact, even if by a miracle he escapes positive error.* It is unnecessary to say that accuracy upon a technical subject is to be preferred to eloquence :

> "* * torrens dicendi copia multis
> Et sua mortifera est facundia."

With this apology for persistent reference to a dry and technical verbiage, let us glance for an instant at the authority of the received terminology, for it is sometimes said that the common law does not pretend to any scientific place in general jurisprudence ; that it is content to be insular rather than catholic, rugged rather than refined, and sensible rather than scientific. But this is to forget that the common law is but a single phase of jurisprudence. In its points of resemblance, the common law responds to the analysis of the elements of jurisprudence ; in its points of difference only is it self-regulating. For more than a hundred years these points of difference and of resemblance have occupied the attention of the English jurisprudents. The speculations of the English, however, have stopped short of the transcendentalism of the Germans, and to-day the English school of jurisprudence is both practical and philosophic, and its teachings of vast importance

---

* As philosophers affirm "that each body of doctrines has its root in some ancestral body of doctrines" (1 Fiske's Cosmic Philos., 166) so, with equal truth lawyers may affirm that each institute of their science has its historical antecedent. Without reference to this history of the philosophy of law, any author, no matter how brilliant his attainment, will fall into sad error while speculating on the genesis of law.

to the reign of law in this country. It is to such men as Hobbes, Bentham, Austin, Maine, Holland, Pollock, Lindley, Markby, Stephen, Digby and Harrison,* that all common lawyers owe a debt of gratitude, for they have placed the common law upon a more highly scientific plane; they have introduced it again to philosophy, from which it has been long separated by archaisms and local accidents; they have fitted it out with definitions and with a terminology which is equal to its most advanced conceptions; they have studied the law of its growth and have extracted the prime factors for general every-day use. It behooves Americans, therefore, unless we desire to stand as the Asiatics toward the attainment of modern legal science, to take note of the labors of this school. In the direction of practical codification, the labors in question are of the utmost importance, for without them we should but imperfectly conceive the subject-matter of codification.

The late eloquent argument by Mr. Carter—and the liberty of using Mr. Carter's name should be pardoned, for he is the spokesman of the opposition—does not conform to the teachings of the scientific jurists. According to this gentleman, codification is concerned with "rules." He states at the outset, "Whoever glances over the varying systems of laws exhibited by civilized States will perceive that in some, as in England and with us, the great body of the rules which determine the rights of men in respect to their persons and their property, have never been directly enacted in a statutory form." This statement, while true, is inexact. The matter with which the jurisprudence of the common law is concerned is law, and law in position, not rules *in posse*. A rule is a very distinct conception from a law, which is a rule plus a sanction, or penalty imposed for its infraction by the supreme political authority. The distinction pointed out may seem hypercritical, but in point of fact it is fundamental, and many of our most erroneous notions regarding codification are directly attributable to its confusion. The faction who regard mere rules, or the nebulous theories of text-writers, as the equivalents of laws set or imposed in one of the authentic legislative

---

* I have included in this enumeration of a few names both the analytical and synthetical, or historical, jurists, for they are closely allied. No science can exist by analysis alone, for analysis is but preparatory to a synthesis of truths.

modes, never can be brought to concede the feasibility of codification. Their conceptions of the subject-matter of codes are too far removed from the plane on which all codification must be based. It is the merit of the dominant English school of jurisprudence that they have caused the distinction noticed to become so apparent that it is now rarely overlooked by modern law-writers. The scientific English jurists thus well exhibit the practical bent of their nation, for recognizing that the limitations of the jurists' law are with man in political societies, their concern with the abstractions concerning law, ends when they cease to be applicable to man in political societies. They define with superlative precision the difference between a rule and a law, and in this respect their analysis has been of service to the cause of codification.

At yet another point does Mr. Carter's opening statement—upon which, by the way, the validity of his entire argument rests—conflict with the discoveries of those whose best energies have been devoted to the analyses of the elements of jurisprudence. He states, in substance, that the systems of law in England and America "rest upon an original but ever-growing body of custom," constantly expounded and amplified by a trained body of experts. But is this statement true?—An unqualified affirmative comes from no school of jurisprudence. The statement is much too broad to receive the assent of the most radical supporter of customary law. The adherents of the potency of customary law may be regarded as of two classes: those who claim that custom, independently of any action of the courts or legislature, has the force of law, and those who assert that the *imprimatur* of the courts must be added to the custom before it attains the force of law, and then that it acts retrospectively. Opposed to these several conceptions are those who deride the very idea of customary law. The adherents of the first class are mainly to be found in Germany. Professor Holland is the best exponent of the second class, as Austin is of the opposition.

No authoritative juridical writer has gone to the extent of asserting with Mr. Carter, that the great body of the private law in England and in America now rests upon custom. This would be far too exclusive a claim for custom. No doubt in certain primitive stages of a nation's growth, as Sir H. Maine's rich and varied experience has enabled him to detect, custom may in itself have the force of law, but in the more advanced stages of a nation, the importance of custom declines until at last there comes a period when all law is written law. It is either written case-law or written statute-law, and when written in a particular way, written code-law.* In this State the development is such that it may well be doubted whether custom is even a source of law except in the single case of the *lex mercatoria* where it is potent only, because, by contract, it is magnified on the mercantile exchanges into prominence. Even if Mr. Carter intended to refer to custom as a source of law, his reference entirely overlooks the fact that custom has never, in this State, been in any way a fertile source of law. For example, the entire body of law promulgated in the courts of equity has in no sense a customary basis. Nor has that residuum of the common law of this State, which is referable to the common law of England, an existence here because of custom ; it is part of the organic law by express constitutional provision.

Having thus roughly pointed out the distinction between custom and law, and between custom as a source of law and as law in itself, the nature of the laws which it is proposed to codify in this State may be briefly summarized : The jurists law is the law evolved either by the supreme legislature or by its ministerial subordinates. The analytical jurists have demonstrated that under any advanced type of government laws are made by the legislature proper and by the various subordinate persons possessing law-making powers. Among the latter persons are the judges who sometimes act in the direct legislative mode, as when they issue what is known as rules of court, and sometimes in the indirect legislative mode, when they state certain principles, independent of the facts *sub judice*. The scope of codification is concerned only with laws evolved by the persons and in the modes indicated, not with custom nor with any of the vague conceptions of those who regard codification of the private law as practically unattainable.

* Maine's Ancient Law, p. 12.

Passing from the consideration of the general to the particular, Mr. Carter's main objections to any codification of the private law of New York may be divided into two classes: first, those which are derived from his reading of history; second, those which he infers from a personal examination of the inherent and the political phases of the common law. Among the first class is the purely negative argument drawn from the failure of England and the various United States to codify their respective private laws, and the consequent presumption against the utility of such codification. Among the second class are the arguments which refer the temporal and the political prosperity of this country and England to the present uncodified condition of the common law. The friends of a better arrangement of the law than that existent do not admit the validity of any of these arguments. Inverting the order of their consideration, we may briefly examine the reasons why this validity is disputed.

If the greatness of the material prosperity of England and this country were in any degree attributable to non-codification of the *ius privatum*, some legitimate argument might be made from the failure referred to. But there is no relation whatever between the facts: when a horse was made consul, Rome enjoyed a system of private law unequaled for wisdom and equity.* Political results depend on the condition of the public law, not on the condition of the private law. It is the nature of its laws and not their codification which either promotes or retards the material prosperity of a State.

Nor can the friends of law reform admit the validity of Mr. Carter's second proposition that codification and absolutism, and non-codification and freedom have any relation whatever. His theory, that non-codification in free States is attributable to the fact that in those States law is evolved from the customs of the people, whereas in monarchical States it is evolved by the crown, is predicated of a misconception of the modes in which laws are made in all States, and in disregard of all that has been written on "sovereignty." As has been already indicated, Germany is the State where the greatest possible

* Phillimore's Disert. on Principles, etc., of jurisp. intd., 1.

force is attributed by jurists to custom, and yet its govern ment can hardly be regarded, according to American notions, as popular. The fact is that the sovereign, be it the people themselves, or be it the most flagrant absolutist, make laws in the same legislative moulds. The legislative power may be distributed differently, but under all types of government, that which pleases the sovereign alone has the force of law. As Mr. Carter repeats: " *Quod principi placuit legis habet vigorem.*" But *principi* in the technical sense means the political sovereign which may be *demos.** If we substitute for *principi* the word *populo*, what terror is there in the ennobled maxim? In this State, where the people make the laws, the people alone codify them, and they are not likely to be frightened by shadows into remaining buried under a mountain of laws, statute and non-statute — a very Pelion on Ossa — because once under other circumstances and conditions a people with a despot had a code.

If it were even true that codification and despotism and non-codification and freedom, are so invariably associated as to convey the idea of cause and effect, a free nation on the eve of codification might well hesitate. But it is not true. Switzer-land and France are republics, and well-ordered examples of enlightened and prosperous States, and there codification flourishes. It is unnecessary to call attention to the invalidity of arguments which fail to be true, when applied to like facts. Another form of this illegitimate argument would permit the allies of codifica-tion to attribute to codification the present blessings of popular government in France. But we know, as Mr. Webster almost prophetically pointed out, in the year 1820, that the present type of government in France is, in all probability, the result of the abolition of primogeniture and of a liberal land tenure.† Mr. Carter's appeal to the patriotic bias thus contains a covert and unjust implication, that in popular States the condition of the law is preferable to that in even the best type of monarchical States; yet in Sweden and in Belgium, for instance, private law is

* Inst. Just., 1, 2, 6. " Sed et quod principi placuit, legis habet vigorem : cum lege regia, quae de imperio eius lata est, populus ei et in eum omne suum imperium et potestatem concessit."
† See note p. 59, vol. 1, Bowen's edit., de Tocqueville's Democ. in America.

administered with fully as much cheapness, dignity and justice as it is here.

The opponents of codification would fain believe that codification is an auxiliary, at least, of despotism, but even this is not inherently true. It is the nature of the laws codified and not codification which is the auxiliary. To amplify Mr. Carter's own similitude, had Mahomet's Koran contained the peaceful tenets of the Divine Nazarene, it could not have aided a dream of human empire. Codification of the trans-Atlantic common law will not debase it. It contains germs which no codification can destroy; excrescences which codification may remove with benefit to the body politic. A code of the private division of the common law will have no effect on the public law, and it is to the public law that we look for our liberties and political rights. Codification of the private law will not affect the constitutions of government, the bicameral legislature, the veto, or the power over the veto, the jury system, the judiciary-establishment working in the inherited common-law mode, the *habeas corpus*, the bill of rights, the inviolability of contracts, the right of compensation for private property arbitrarily taken, or successions *ab intestato*, including the abolition of primogeniture, and unless these things are affected, by what authority is it intimated that liberties will be endangered by a more compact form of the private, as contradistinguished from the public, law? Mr. Carter's argument upon this point may not have been serious, it having been intimated, by a clever reviewer, that in this particular the danger feared from codification, had some reference to the votes of the bucolic constituencies. Notwithstanding this intimation it has been assumed that the danger in question is honestly apprehended by Mr. Carter, and issue has been taken accordingly with some degree of seriousness.

It is likewise urged against a codification of the private division of the common law that it will have a tendency to increase injustice by reason of an augmented judicial inclusion of cases not within the purview of the codified law; or else, that the struggle of the judges to exempt from the operation of the Code a case presenting distinctive features will be productive of an increased uncertainty in legal administration. These alternative and inconsistent propositions are old phases of the argument against the so-called rigidity of statute law. It will be observed that they postulate a considerable inefficiency on the part of the judiciary as well as in the qualities of statute law. If it is true that in one or other of these propositions lies the whole philosophy of codification, the question is a narrow one. Those who affirm the superiority of an orderly arrangement of a jurisprudence deny that a code increases the proportion of injustice in the given case, if at all, to such an extent as to outweigh the benefits to be derived from the added certainty and the compactness of expression found in a code. In stating this proposition it must not be forgotten that it has no reference to criminal administration which is embraced in the division, public law. In any system of private law there can be no greater evil than uncertainty and in any system of public law, no greater evil than injustice. The assumption that the judges will increase the proportion of error by the inclusion of exceptional cases within the common provisions of a code is unwarranted. The administration of law is usually a struggle to include the contested case within a certain law, whether that law has emanated from the superior legislative body, or from the inferior legislative body—the judiciary. The interpreting function of a court is always either restrictive or extensive, and if it err in the performance of this function, the proper checks still exist by means of appeals. Because of codification, the judicial operations do not change : with a fearless bar and an intelligent judiciary, there will be in the future, as in the past, the same effort to arrive at exact justice, the same effort to distinguish the given case and possibly as great a proportion of error, though it is thought not. Yet the question of codification lies deeper than either of these arguments, being, whether the sum of all the advantages to be derived from codification is not greater than the sum of all the disadvantages in remaining without a code?—Mr. Carter nowhere alludes to the side of the advantages which at a later stage will be outlined in this paper.

After brief allusion to those parts of the common law which have been already codified, and the qualified admission that so far codes answer very well, Mr. Carter arraigns any codification of that arbitrary division, known as the private law, as unscientific

in theory. This accusation is only perceived, in all its ful-
ness, by employing antithetical modes in stating it. It must
mean that the present arrangement of the private division of
the common law is superior to that proposed, or else that no
new and better arrangement is attainable. That the arrangement
in a code is the less scientific one, is then sought to be demonstrated
by the proposition, that the private department of the common
law is now embodied in the reports of adjudications, which are so
provisional in their nature as not to be disembarrassed from the
particular groupings of fact on which their elements depend.
The answer to this half-truth necessitates a reference to the mode
in which the judicial branch of government works. A judge
in the decision of a case decides, it is true, only the special case
before him, but it is the practice among the common-law judges
to formulate the reasons for this adjudication. Those reasons
which turn upon the isolated facts of a given case rarely have any
future value, for the facts of any two cases are seldom the same.
But in the reasons which are independent of the particular
facts, jurisprudents detect a law, technically termed the *ratio
decidendi**. *Ratio decidendi* must not be confused with *dicta*,
which are unauthoritative special references to facts, nor with
ratio legis, which is another thing. These general statements of principles independent of the particular groupings
of fact, are operative as laws, but as laws standing out of true
position in some old or new chronicle of judicial work, termed
reports. Piled up in all manner of volumes, thousands upon
thousands, are these isolated, illogical and fragmentary laws.
Now the adherents of codification simply insist that these
dispersed expressions of substantive law are susceptible of
being selected by skilful and logical persons, and when selected of being classified, their inconsistencies and redundan-
cies being first expunged. Certainly in common practice the
lawyer examines the reports with the view of ascertaining the
law of his case: he rejects the dissimilarities of fact and he
extracts the law which is always true. If the lawyer after his
examination of the reports were to give a provisional opinion as

* 2 Austin's Jurisp., 330: Holland's Jurisp.; Pollock's essay "Science of Case Law"
passim.

to the law, his client would certainly be justified in promising a provisional fee. What the lawyer does in his daily practice, the codifier does on a larger scale; both seek for the law in the reports, but in the reports unfortunately burdened with the scholia of the text-writers and with the wearisome utterance of many a common-place or undiscriminating official. When the codifier has found these laws, he lodges them between single covers that common people, and not logicians and experts alone, may better apply them to the myriad, shifting phases of human affairs.

One thoughtless answer to this account of the task of the codifier is that every good lawyer knows these general principles, these larger expressions of substantive law, and that it is superfluous to codify such vague generalities. But this assumption is contrary to the fact; no human mind is capable of systematically producing off-hand the several thousand basic principles usually stated in a code of private law. Yet if it is otherwise, their codification is a duty which the State owes to the less gifted portion of its citizens; to those who cannot remember even a hundred principles, as well as to those who are not conversant with law at all.

Another answer denies with eager confidence the teachings of the scientific jurists, that judiciary-made-law is in reality legislation, and that judicial bodies are to be classified with legislatures. Mr Carter pronounces it "a shallow view," because the freedom of action is, he thinks, the final test of the legislative power and the judges are non-free. But if freedom of action were the final test of legislative power, the legislatures of constitutional States would lack this supreme qualification. In England and in America, legislatures are not free; they are fettered by fundamental restrictions, by common-law rules of parliamentary procedure, analogous to the rules of practice of judiciary bodies as well as by the inherent forces of the common law in all its entirety; their freedom of action is but negative, consisting in the power not to act, or not to act in a particular way; they cannot substitute caprice for duty or the positively wrong for the positively right. Freedom of action, then, is not the finality of legislative power. There have been times, indeed, when the assertion by the

2

judiciary of freedom of action almost transcends any like assertion of the legislature proper; for example, the conduct of the court of chancery after the passage of the Statute of Uses.* The test of the legislative power is not freedom of action in the law maker, but the power to pronounce what shall be law, and the power to impose a sanction for the future infraction of this law.

There is another error which is made by the opponents of codification, as it seems to those who view codes favorably; namely, the assumption that a complete code must embrace a statutory statement of the thousands of decisions predicated of peculiar groupings of fact. A true system of codification is concerned only with those larger principles indicated; those which have the force of law universally, or independently of the peculiar groups of facts to which they have, or have not, been applied. When we reflect that already many of these decisions have been transmuted into statutes and that the rest are embodied in leading cases, the final arbitraments of the courts of last resort, we recognize the limitations of the codifier's work, and that it is within an attainable compass.

Yet granting this last fact, the iteration of the cherished idea of the opponents of codes, that codification will destroy the elasticity of the common law, deters some persons from favoring codification. By elasticity in law is probably meant the facile applicability of laws to new groups of fact. In this idea the scientific jurists detect a fallacy, a confusion between the " *terminus a quo* and the *terminus ad quem* of codification. Because codification defines the general principles from which all legal arguments start— the *terminus a quo*—it is not necessarily true that it defines the *terminus ad quem*, the extent of the application of which these principles are susceptible."† In simpler language, the error in question consists in assuming that the Code provides for all cases and that new difficulties, clearly beyond the equity of the statute, will be dealt with improperly. If codification were to put an end to the proper solution of new difficulties, or to circumscribe the common law judicial powers, we might well pause before entering

---

* Taltarum's case (Year Book. 12 Ed., iv., 19) may also be cited.
† Holland's Form of the Law, p. 57.

upon a systematic codification. There is, however, no such danger to be apprehended. The judicial process of evolving new law by cross-application of old laws has been going on in all States ever since the primitive times when their judicial branches of government were separated from the executive. The archæologists, who have as intimate an acquaintance with dead nations as those nations ever had with themselves, show that the Assyrian judges were diligent searchers of the Akkadian law reports of hundreds of years before, and therefore, that the process of extracting new law by cross-application, and by the *ratio decidendi* is as old as anything we know of judicial proceedings.* It is fair to presume that in the future, as in the past, this purely logical process will not cease unless we concede a boundary to mental activities.

There is no insurmountable difficulty in codifying private law, and by private law is meant that which Mr. Carter himself would seem to consider private law in a division of any body of law into public and private. It must be borne in mind that this division of law into public and private, is purely scholastic or fanciful; the Germans include in private law, the law of crimes, and to them public law means *Staatsrecht*, or constitutional law. Mr. Carter's ingenuous statement, that he is not aware that the distinction between public and private law has hitherto been dwelt upon in the discussion concerning codification, contains a singular admission. The one distinction never lost sight of in any systematic view, or arrangement, of a body of law is this very division into public and private law. It is the basis of Holland's great contribution to jurisprudence which though not entitled a work on codification is generally recognized as the ablest presentation of that view which would make rights, and not duties, the basis of a scientific codification.† If we run the division line of law into public and private where Mr. Carter would place it, there is no more difficulty in codifying the law on the one side of the division than there would be in codifying the law on the other side of

---

* The Akkadians, or Accadians, occupied much the same relation to the Assyrians in literature, language and art that ancient Rome bears to the modern Romance nations. The record of decisions of the Akkadian judges seems to have been preserved upon clay rolls engraved with a style.

† Chap. 6, part 1, Wise's Outlines of Jurisp.

this arbitrary line. The difficulty supposed is referable entirely to indistinct conceptions of the scope of codification and of its true limitations. It has never been claimed for any modern code, much less for the Civil Code of New York, that it was to be the exclusive repository of all private law, past, present and future. No code can ever accomplish so great a task, and any attempt to accomplish it will prove a disastrous failure. What has been claimed for the Civil Code of New York may be referred to when Mr. Carter's special pleas against all codification have been first noticed.

The great force of the example of those nations which have already resorted to codification is always sought to be broken by the enemies of codes. While the form of their arguments differ, they almost invariably concede something to the historical parallels, for such the example of those nations may be regarded. Mr. Carter, insisting that the example of Rome in particular is, in no degree, illustrative of present exigencies in the State of New York, is, however, unwilling to concede the usual modicum.

Any attempt at a philosophical consideration of the Roman law is no light matter. It is usually regarded as an *adytum* which those who are not votaries do not disturb. But the rule in this respect having been ruthlessly broken by the inference indicated, it may with some propriety be diffidently submitted that the highest modern authorities do not coincide with Mr. Carter's deductions from the example of Rome. Even Gibbon, whose masterly analysis of the purely external phases of Roman law is familiar to most educated people, affords slender basis for the extreme deductions of Mr. Carter, and since Gibbon's famous chapter,[1] a careful and minute modern scholarship[2] has elucidated the jurisprudence of Rome, in a manner Gibbon but faintly conceived.[3] A nation's law is so entirely the expression and result of its peculiar civilization, that to be studied with success it must be studied historically. This is especially true of Roman law, for the *Corpus iuris civilis*

---

[1] Written *circiter*, A. D. 1784.
[2] The institutes of Gaius were discovered by Niebuhr in 1816. Even Gibbon's famous arrangement of the eras of Roman law, followed by Hugo, is now altered.
[3] Tomkins and Jencken's Modern Rom. Law, Pref. xi.

is an historical document ; [1] Mr. Carter has recognized this fact
and has outlined rapidly the place which he conceives the Justinian compilations [2] occupy in the history of Rome. For this
purpose he begins with the Code of the Decemvirs, and intimates
that this early specimen of the codification of private law was
found so inelastic that it was subtly evaded by the fictions of
the praetors and by the operations of the professional jurists.
Whence he deduces, that all codification of private law must
prove a failure. He likewise intimates that the Justinian compilations, when analyzed, furnish no adequate data in support of
the proposed codification of the private law of New York. The
various positions of his argument are, however, too familiar to
need a preliminary repetition.

In order to ascertain whether the Decemviral Code was, as
Mr. Carter's argument plainly infers, an error in the policy of
Roman legal development we must recall the facts which com-
pose its environment. The literary world was first enabled to
penetrate that historical *nox arcana*, the kingly period of Roman
history, by the genius of Barthold Niebuhr, but since his day a
flood of light has been thrown upon the early history of Italy,
and now its monuments stand forth with clearness and in some
sort of perspective. Yet the clearness is still comparative,
clouded, as it were, with enigma, or with that dim obscurity which
must to some extent envelop a pre-historic age. Not only the
origin of the Decemviral Code is uncertain, but even its contents,
two-thirds of it only having been restored from scattered fragments by the labors of the exegetical and the historical jurists.
Whatever its dubious origin may have been, this primitive code
contains little or no argument either for or against modern codification, although it is a most potent witness to the advantages of
fixity and certainty in the basis of a nation's jurisprudence.
The Decemviral Code contained the germs of the private, as well

[1] Intd. Cumin's Civ. Law.
[2] In deference to Professor Amos' criticism (repeated by Mr. Carter) of Mr. Field's introduction to the Civil Code, I have refrained from using the "Code Justinian" as a convenient
English designation for the entire *Corpus Iuris*. I do not, however, mean to be understood as
assenting to the propriety of Prof. Amos' criticism. Mr. Field's deference to popular, rather
than to technical custom, is habitual with him and in the use of the "Code Justinian" as *nomen
collectivum* of the entire *Corpus Iuris*, Institutes, Digest, Code and Novells, he has the sanction
of Austin, Story and other writers who certainly knew what every lawyer knows that the
Corpus Iuris does not consist of the code alone.

as of the public, law of Rome. *Fons omnis publici privatique iuris*,[1] Livy called it, and **Professor Moyle** has lately said of it, " that English lawyers in particular will fully appreciate the advantage which was secured by this expression of the law in a more scientific and therefore convenient form than that in which it had hitherto been clothed."[2] Mommsen speaks of it as " an invaluable basis,"[3] and certainly no further testimony to the wisdom of its inception can be necessary. The tenacity with which the Romans clung to this basis of their national law is one of the most extraordinary facts in the history of jurisprudence, and it is surely incorrect to refer its gradual subsidence to the mal-adaptation to human needs of written law.

For the purpose of indicating the error contained in the assumption that the Decemviral Code was ultimately swept away, because written law was too inelastic to be readily suited to the practical work of administering justice, let us briefly review the leading facts connected with it : In the one thousand years which elapsed between the Decemviral Code and the compilations of Justinian, an insignificant community had become, step by step, first the Italian hegemony and finally the monarch of the world, but with Theodosius the supremacy of Rome began to decline although its power and influence were destined to survive through its laws. It is instructive that through all this vast cycle of rise, conquest and decline, the Decemviral Code remained the basis of Roman jurisprudence. It is not surprising that a code well adapted to Latium should, ultimately, in the course of centuries, fail to respond to the needs of a vast empire ; nor, is it strange that laws well suited to a primitive tribe should fall short of meeting all the multitudinous requirements of a growing and progressive nation. Yet so persistently were the Romans in favor of the stability of law that they preserved the letter of their first code after edictal legislation had swept its substance away. At the time of the promulgation of the code of the first decemvirate (b. c. 451), the territorial dominion of that we now call Rome, in obedience to later dictates, was insignifi-

---

[1] Livy III. 31.
[2] Imperatoris Iustiniani Institutiones, Moyle. Intd. 14.
[3] 1 Mommsen's Rome, 367.

cant; the last Veientine war had not even been fought. But in Cicero's day (B. C. 100) the entire Mediterranean was within Roman territory; the legionaries had triumphed throughout Macedonia and Greece, in Asia and in Africa and in Hispania to the Pillars of Hercules, the gate of the ancient unknown. The crowds of foreigners who had meanwhile swarmed to the Roman hive, necessitated changes in the early law, for the *ius civile* had no reference to strangers. Consequently the prætor peregrinus, a kind of magistrate having jurisdiction over foreigners, was established (B. C. 247). This prætorship as well as the older one, the urban prætorship, the aediles, the pro-consuls and the pro-prætors each possessed the power of legislation, *ius edicendi*[1], a subdivision of the kingly function. The prætor did not sit as judge at a Roman trial; he acted as the president of the court, but had no voice in the sentence; he had the *imperium* but not the *jurisdictio*. By these authorities it was that the primitive law was enabled to be subjected to those impulses which ultimately greatly changed its constituency, if not its form.

To attribute the almost imperceptible repeal or subsidence of the Decemviral Code to judicial action is to misapprehend a curious phase of Roman legal development. It has not always been the case that the legislative powers have been separated from the other powers of government. In primitive and archaic types of government very strange distributions of governmental power have taken place. Modern conceptions, it must not be forgotten, rarely apply to ancient institutions: To those familiar with the brief and recent constitutional history of the Province of New York, this fact will be readily apparent, for prior to the war-for-independence, the crown-governor possessed and asserted legislative, as well as judicial and executive, powers.[2]

The fact that a species of legislation and not judicial impulse was the great power which gradually changed the early Roman law, as first expressed in its primitive code, is not inconsistent with that other fact which Sir H. Maine has made so familiar to us all, that fiction is one of the great elements of change in

[1] *Ius edicere* was to declare the law in a general manner; *ius dicere* was to organize the formula.
[2] The present jurisdiction of the Supreme Court of New York, is largely derived from an edict of governor, Lord Bellomont, promulgated in 1699.

the rigidity of any particular body of law. By fiction, however, this great writer means something quite different from that which an English-speaking lawyer ordinarily means. He means any false assumption of fact made by a magistrate.[1] Whether the magistrates in the case of Rome acted judicially or as legislators when they resorted to particular fictions, Professor Maine does not always stop to particularize, though he would himself sharply discriminate between the several functions. It is unquestionably true that the prætors and the other Roman magistrates frequently resorted to fictions as the *ratio legis* embodied in their *edicta*, and that even Gaius does not always recognize these edicts as types of legislative acts.[2] But in the days of Gaius, jurisprudence had not attained to that philosophic analysis of its elements which is the distinguishing feature of the higher jurisprudence of this day.[3]

It is hardly possible in any rapid survey of the development of Roman private law during so long a period as one thousand years, to summarize, as Mr. Carter has done, conditions by general statements of fact. What is true of to-day fails to be true of to-morrow. Mr. Carter has given prominence to what he regards as an historical fact, that the greatest development of Roman private law was due to an unofficial lawyer-class, and not to the usual law-making or legislative powers of government. He regards the Roman magistrates as ephemeral politicians, dominated by the lawyers of the day, and in these respects he recognizes a likeness to the unsystematic development of the private division of the jurisprudence of English-speaking peoples. If this hypothesis is true, any systematic improvement in the law of Rome was due not to the State but to the chance interference of the jurisconsults, an unofficial class of law-makers as Mr. Carter would have us believe. This mere re-statement of the moral Mr. Carter's argument tends to convey, shows that it appears to be based, nay, is based, upon a misconception of the modes in which the development of the private law of Rome actually occurred. No doubt

---

[1] Ancient Law, p. 24.
[2] Poste's Gaius, 36.
[3] "In the systematic exhibition of the law, the Romans were, comparatively speaking, very feeble. In this respect they are greatly excelled by the moderns."—Tompkins' Inst. of Rom. Law, Part I. p. 105.

the jurisconsults were a powerful element in this development, but they were an element which the State ultimately converted into a legislative element, nurturing and directing it so as to adapt it to public purposes. Nor, is it more true that the regular law-making power of the Roman State was in any considerable degree in the hands of evanescent or incompetent politicians who were dominated wholly by lawyers. Sir H. Maine, an authority who may be trusted, says the prætor himself was generally a jurist. Certainly Papinian held high public office under Marcus Aurelius and both Ulpian and Paulus were among other things prætorian prefects when that office was largely civil in character, while Quintus Mucius Scævola, the founder of scientific jurisprudence, was consul[1] in the year B. C. 95. Undoubtedly at every stage of Roman history there were jurists who were prætors, just as there were prætors who were both politicians and jurists. In this respect the development of Roman law was not, according to American standards, abnormal. There is one phase, then, in the development of Roman private law which Mr. Carter's paper does not emphasize, although it is important in view of the relation it bears to the Justinian compilations. I refer to the extraordinary legislative power transferred by the Roman State to the jurisconsults.[2]

The craft of Augustus, who found it impossible to destroy the influence of the jurisconsults, suggested a way in which this powerful order might be allied to the new imperial system.[3] Prior to this time, the *responsa* or opinions of the jurisconsults had great authority but no binding force as law.[4] Unless we understand the change Augustus instituted by this remarkable delegation of the legislative power to certain learned men, we shall unhappily miss one of the great features in the development of the jurisprudence of Rome. Mommsen, generalizing in this connection, says : " Apart from the more general political conditions on which jurisprudence also, and indeed jurisprudence especially depends, the causes of the excellence of the Roman civil law lie mainly in two features : first, that the plaintiff and defendant were specially

---

[1] The functions of consuls differed greatly at different epochs.
[2] Dig. 1, 2, 47.
[3] Imperatoris Iustiniani Inst.; Moyle's Intd., 50.
[4] Mackeldey's Rom. Law, 21.

obliged to explain and embody in due and binding form, the grounds of the demand and of the objections to comply with it ; and secondly, that the Romans appointed a permanent machinery for the edictal development of their law, and associated it immediately with practice * * * * by the latter they prevented incapable law-making so far as such things can be prevented at all."[1]

Notwithstanding Mommsen's eulogium of Roman methods of legislation, and there can be none higher, it may, at this point, well be doubted whether the lawyer-class of a State make the safest body of legislators, and whether they are even through the regular channels of their avocation, the best means of developing a grand system of jurisprudence. The functions of the scientific legislator are not seldom confused with those which pertain to the lawyer as such, and yet they are most distinct. It is a common opinion among people who are not lawyers—and they argue that for every lawyer there are a million other men—that the notions of most lawyers are by professional habit too circumscribed to enable them to take wide or beneficent views of matters not immediately within the narrow range of their little personal activities.[2] But it is unfair to thus generalize, for the exceptions to this questionable rule have been so frequent; although, on the other hand, it is manifestly most fair that the beautiful picture, which Mr. Carter has drawn for us, of the development of law by a trained lawyer-class only, should be so stated that all sides of a public question may be properly considered.

Continuing the discussion concerning the *iuris consulti* and the nature of their influence on Roman law, it will be recalled that even before the time of Augustus their then unauthentic *responsa* had become so diffuse that Julius Cæsar, as well as Cicero, had perceived the necessity of some sort of redaction by eliminating the parts of the smallest value. After Augustus a like difficulty arose with the *responsa signata*, the now *quasi-legislative* acts of the authorized jurists. The contrariety and opposition of so many individual law-givers began to be confusing

---

[1] Mommsen's Rome, 555.
[2] Herbert Spencer's Sociology, " Class Bias," 241.

to legal administration. Hadrian added to the confusion by giving the force of law to the writings of the systematic writers. Several attempts were made to remedy the confusion incidental to this type of laws, and in A. D. 426 the law which Hugo called the "citation law," was issued by the Emperors Theodosius II. and Valentinian III., declaring that the majority of the opinions of the authorized jurists should thereafter determine the law, and that when they were equal, Papinianus should prevail : "*Ubi autem diversæ sentiæ proferuntur, potior numerus vincat auctorem, vel si numerus aequalis sit, ejus partis præcedat auctoritas in qua excellent isingenii vir Papinianus emineat, etc.*" There is some dispute among the critical as to whether in fact this "law of Citations" did, as Gibbon states, and Mr. Carter after him, have the effect of reducing the number of the *iuris auctores* to five, Gaius, Papinian, Ulpian, Paulus and Modestinus. There is a *posteriori* authority for inferring that such could not have been the intention of the " law of Citations," for Justinian's Constitution, in reference to the compilation of the Digest, instructs the compilers to make excerpts from the authorized jurists only, and acting under this commission the compilers actually selected thirty-nine.[1]

Without venturing further into the precincts of those competent to express opinions upon such delicate questions as that just noticed, enough may now have been stated to show that the private law of Rome was most influenced by written law, but by written law of a peculiar type, and that its development was not abandoned by the State wholly to chance or to the whim of those who chose to play, dilettante-fashion, with the development of private law. From the time of the last rescript, the "law of Citations," to the reign of Justinian, in the Eastern Empire, was little over a hundred years, and during this period matters went from bad to worse : it was the reign of diabolical confusion by reason of the great wealth of authority which the parties-litigant might cite upon any shade of legal discussion. This confusion was augmented by the continued irregular extensions of the Constitutions to those departments of law which had been

---

[1] Imperatoris Iustiniani Inst., Moyle's Intd., 59.

formed by the *responsa prudentium* and the *sensentiæ* of the systematic writers, the *iuris auctores*. One law-making power thus clashed with another. Constantine had put an end to the prætorian function of harmonizing the principles of law and equity ; the medium of making law by the *responsa* of the jurisprudents, had died with Maximian (*circ*. A. D. 305), so that imperial legislation at last became the only medium by which changes could be effected in the positive law.[1] The mass of the Constitutions, as the laws emanating directly from the Emperor himself were called, soon became very great. Various attempts between the time of Constantine and that of Justinian had been made to systematically compile these Constitutions, notably the *Codex Gregorianus* (*circ*. A. D. 295), the *Codex Hermogenianus* (*circ*. A. D. 365, 398) and the *Codex Theodosianus* (*circ*. A. D. 439). Still these statutes multiplied. Justinian's reform was intended to remedy the confusion in both branches of the *ius scriptum* and to harmonize the Constitutions with that system of pseudo-statutes which had been promulgated through the medium of the *responsa* and *sententiæ* of the jurists.[2] This task was accomplished to some extent in the *Pandects*. It is not necessary to repeat wel. known details concerning the precise nature of the material composing Justinian's compilations. The result has been applauded from the revival of learning until the present day, and it would be a curious idiosyncrasy to attempt to take a new view of so meritorious a performance, comparatively speaking, as the *Corpus iuris civilis*. Enough has, perhaps, been stated to base a conclusion quite at variance with that which the reader must arrive at after a perusal of Mr. Carter's survey of the same work, and no more has been attempted.

To attribute to Justinian any imperialistic scheme in the law reform which he completed is to be at variance with opposite deductions which may be made from the same state of facts. Theodosius and others had designed to undertake this very reform in a spirit which cannot be questioned ; so that we must always postulate the necessity of reform even when we imagine the motive of Jus-

---

[1] Moyle's Inst. Intd. 57, *et passim*.
[2] There is an abundance of authority for regarding the dogma of the jurists as translated into statutes at certain epochs of Roman history. See Poste's Gaius, pp. 37, 144, for ready reference, though, indeed, not the most apposite.

tinian in executing it to have been sinister. But all the arguments which those in favor of codification draw from the Justinian compilations are quite opposed to those Mr. Carter would wish to draw. The Pandects did embrace the private law of the Eastern empire in an authoritative legislative version and to this extent it is illustrative of the present purpose in New York. That the Pandects do not respond to modern notions of statutes is hardly argumentative when we consider that the *responsa* and *sententiæ* of which the Pandects were composed, were not themselves in the form of statutes, though they became operative as statutes; '*legis vicem obtinent.*' This is but another instance of .the necessity of considering that laws in all ages are not expressed in the same modes and that formerly they were not habitually expressed in imperative terms. Nor, is it strange that Justinian's collaborateurs, in arranging the Pandects, adhered to the ancient form of the *sententiæ* and *responsa*, preferring to leave them what they always had been, after the State had officially ratified them, statutes in effect but not in form or expression. It is not necessary to point out to any one familiar with the discussion that this plan was adopted only after mature consideration.

In reality there is no connection between the fall of Rome and the redaction and consolidation of the Roman law under Justinian. The universal *imperium* of Rome had departed long before Justinian, the empire having been divided in A. D. 395, more than a hundred years before that barbarian Sclav had ascended the throne. Justinian's subjects, whatever they were, were not Roman. To any true lover of Gibbon's masterpiece its very title conveys the fact that Rome had fallen before the Justinian era began. Another great English historian has beautifully pointed out the extreme difficulty in determining when Roman history ends, it glided so imperceptibly into the Middle Ages, but the vulgar and therefore the more conspicuous boundary, is placed in A. D. 476, some fifty years before Justinian's great reform.

A word upon the duration of Justinian's redaction of the ancient private law of Rome, and this branch of the subject, already unjustifiably long, may be abandoned to those whose tastes and acquirements are adapted to its discussion. The authorities are not at one upon the statement, early made by its enemies, that the *Corpus iuris civilis* was soon either ignored or superseded by its contemporaries and their successors. Ever since its promulgation there has been an anti-Justinian party, opposed to the work which Justinian wrought. By them it was first asserted that, in some respects, Justinian himself superimposed amendments upon the *Corpus iuris civilis* from motives of mercenary traffic in justice. But other persons, fortunately for human nature, deny this to be the fact. That the *Corpus iuris civilis* was soon ignored or superseded, is also at issue, and it is doubtful whether Professor Hadley's interesting lectures, delivered before the undergraduates of Yale and full of striking antitheses calculated to arrest their attention, are entitled to be regarded by Mr. Carter as the controlling authority upon this point. Professor Hadley himself never published his lectures and was not regarded as a high authority upon Roman law. But if he is adequate authority, he is not confirmed in this statement by Savigny, Mackeldey, Ortolan, deFerrière, Cumins, or Tomkins, still higher authorities upon this branch of the history of Roman law. By these last-named writers it is asserted that the *Corpus iuris* of Justinian maintained its legal effect with very little variation for at least six hundred years after its promulgation. The manner in which it finally became the basis of the modern law of Europe, Savigny has fully revealed to students of jurisprudence and many lay-writers to the world at large.

Notwithstanding their debt to the Civil Law, the English-speaking lawyers alone have been tardy in paying their reckoning to the most scientific source of the common law; and yet there have always been exceptions to this rule. The merits of the *Corpus iuris* and its important relations to the Anglican common law were notably conceded by Dr. Duck in 1649,[1] a concession subsequently assailed with great virulence. Sir William Jones, whose fame as a scholar increases daily, termed it "the source of all our English laws that were not of feudal origin."[2] Ample amends are now being made in England for past neglect. The late edition of Bracton's Commentaries published under the

[1] Duck's *de authoritate juris civilis*, Lib. II. Cap. VIII.
[2] Lord Teignmouth's Memoirs of Sir Wm. Jones, Vol. II., p. 108.

direction of the Master of the Rolls and edited by Sir Travers
Twiss has enabled American lawyers to have easy access to a
fundamental treatise of the common law, but the common law
identical with the Roman law. Savigny is said to have derived
great assistance from Bracton in writing his "History of the
Roman law in the Middle Ages."[1] Through Professor Güter-
bock's work on Bracton's relations to the Roman law, familiar to
most Americans in consequence of Mr. Brinton Coxe's excellent
Philadelphia edition, we had long known the resemblance Bracton bore to Azo's Summa on the Code and Institutes of Justinian, but in Sir Travers Twiss' edition of Bracton we have the
parallel text. It is too late to maintain that any mere arrangement of a private law of a civilized nation contains more political
danger than another arrangement of the same law. Danger lies
below the surface. If any lesson whatever is to be drawn by us
in New York from the consolidation of the Roman law under
Justinian, it is, as Mr. Field has asserted, favorable to a codification of the law of New York. That the compilations of Justinian differ wholly from modern English conceptions of codification
cannot be denied. Their lack of scientific arrangement was so
great that Leibnitz proposed to re-arrange [2] the entire *Corpus
iuris* and Pothier earned the title of *pandectarum restitutor feli-
cissimus* by his re-arrangement of the Pandects. It would be
extremely curious if the codal legislation of another age and
nation could serve as a model for this country of to-day. Yet, as
will hereafter be pointed out, Mr. Field has not substituted novel
arrangements where several ages and nations have demonstrated
the utility of a particular model. In this respect he is at variance
with the radical notions of several amateur codifiers.

It is, no doubt, unnecessary to attempt to refute in detail the
too wide assertions, that the modern specimens of codification,
adopted by France and Germany, are practical failures, and that
the motive which led to their adoption was purely dynastic or
imperialistic but not reformatory; for if these assertions had con-
formed wholly to the facts they would not be even argumentative of the result or motive which attends codification in this

---

[1] Tomkins' Inst. Rom. Law, Intd. 2, note.
[2] Leibnitz, Nova Methodus Discend. et Docend. Iuris. Pars II, c. 85, 90.

State. Yet as such assertions when uttered by a gifted and respected lawyer of mature experience may be damaging to the pending reform, it is proper to supply certain facts in this connection which are not noticed in the course of Mr. Carter's paper, premising the argument upon the historical parallels is by no means a new one in code-discussion, having been repeatedly and exhaustively made upon all sides.

Codification in France, while accomplished under the First Napoleon, had been mooted at intervals from the reign of Louis XI. At the time it was adopted the measure had long had the sanction of French jurists and statesmen, owing to the fact that in France prior to 1789 there was such an immense number of separate systems of jurisprudence as to fairly justify Voltaire's *mot*,[1] that a traveler in that country was compelled to change laws as often as he changed horses. This fact, as well as the careful and scientific mode in which Napoleon caused the commission, appointed for the purpose, to investigate the entire subject of codification, and the subsequent discussion which ensued upon every sentence of the French codes,[2] preclude the attribution of sinister motives only to Napoleon's protectorate of the French codes. The assertion that the French codes were imperialistic in design, tendency and character was long ago made and refuted in this State. In 1814, Mr. Rodman, then a prominent member of the metropolitan bar, stated in an introduction to his edition of the Commercial Code of France, as follows : " The notion entertained by many people in this country that this system of laws " (the French) " is wholly founded upon arbitrary power and consequently affords no security to the rights of persons or the enjoyment of property is equally erroneous and absurd * * * * The excellence of laws as they respect the mutual relations and the multifarious commerce of men in society depends much more upon the enlightened views and the wisdom of the lawyers than upon the nature of the government or the freedom of the people."

It may be quite true that the French have not, as asserted by some writers, hit upon the best plan of codification and that the

[1] Encyc. Brit. Tit. "Codes."
[2] *Motifs et Discours du Code Civil.*

separation of the laws relating to commerce is a deviation from logical methods of codification, and yet there are reasons for concluding that the supposed scientific tests do not all apply to France by reason of local conditions not fully observed by the scientific writers. One reason for the latter conclusion is that the French codes have proved most satisfactory in the actual administration of the French system of laws. Another reason, pointing in the same direction, is that the French codes have taken deep hold in most of the European countries adjacent to France. The Italian government, to the conceded fairness of whose jurists this country frequently appeals, has lately adopted, with some modifications, the French codes. In a consideration of the French codes it is not safe to rely, as Mr. Carter does, upon isolated English opinion. The American authorities upon the merits of the French codes, such as Edward Everett, for some time minister to France, and John Rodman, whose *magnum opus* was a translation of these very codes, are certainly quite equal in this respect to either Austin or Amos, quoted by Mr. Carter. Mr. Rodman's candid verdict, after a most minute examination of the entire text, was embodied in these words "the code Napoleon is unquestionably a work of the highest merit, whether we consider the pure morality, the sound legal principles and enlightened reason which pervade every part of it, or the lucid order, precision and method with which the matter is arranged and exhibited."[1] It is impossible to concede, in view of the remark lately made by an English barrister, Mr. Mosely, in the London Law Magazine and Review,[2] that the state of the French law has received considerable attention in England, or even enough to enable a foreigner to speak with authority upon its inherent forces and defects. Mr. Mosely states : " It is a fact not to be ignored that in carrying on the amendments of our law (in England) too little regard has hitherto been paid to those systems which prevail amongst continental nations, and in this respect our legal reformers have justly laid themselves open to comment." He proceeds to designate the points in the French administration of law which are superior to the English.

---

[1] Rodman's Com. Code of France. Such also was Edward Everett's verdict, 20 N. A. Review, 393.
[2] November, 1883.

Not only is it doubtful whether the motive of the French codification is correctly surmised by Mr. Carter, but whether the complaints, quoted by him, concerning the state of juristic literature in France after the codes, are well founded. Both Austin and Amos, who originally made the complaints in question, seem to have overlooked the fact that when any body of law is systematized the inevitable tendency of juristic literature is to take the form of a commentary on the code. The motive for the great number of special treatises on various topics ceases, and literary activity naturally addresses itself to the actual state of the law. Such was the tendency largely among the Romans after the edict had been consolidated and such has been the case in France since the adoption of the codes. Writers in favor of codification see in this literary tendency a very great advantage and not the disadvantage prophesied by Mr. Carter, the extinction of the "gladsome light of jurisprudence" as he poetically phrases it. That codification would extinguish all but the considerable institutional treatises of the common law is possible, but it is feared not probable ; existing works are too full of concrete examples. But should all but a score of the legal treatises, produced in the last century in the United States, disappear forever, no irremediable harm would be done. Chancellor Kent when asked what made him a great lawyer is said to have epigrammatically replied " lack of law books." When his career began books were comparatively few but these he knew well.[1] Another of New York's great lawyers is said never to have used any but old editions of the treatise-writers, preferring to split hairs for himself from general principles and not from the concrete instances of application given by the editors. At present, as Mr. Pollock has said, there are a number of treatises upon the common law, good, bad and indifferent, overlapping each other, defying all system, and entirely omitting many things we desire to know. The advantage of a new departure will be that the time of the writer " now devoted to a laborious and often barren collection of authorities will be left free for rational explanation." Mr. Carter is quite too sanguine if he has the slightest apprehension that

---

[1] Chancellor Kent's fancy for the text of the *Corpus juris civilis* and his dislike of its modern commentators were also freely avowed in a letter to Mr. Schmit.

juristic literature, such as we have, will "wither." The only change that may possibly come to it by the contemplated alterations in the form of the law must be for the better, and in the direction of that system and elegance which all persons, except some "case-fettered" lawyers, concede to be the present charac-teristic of most American and English law books.[1]

A comparatively recent writer in the Scottish Journal of Jurisprudence[2] enables the English reader to detect that the argument against the motive, character and result of codification in Germany is also unsound. This writer deplores the lack of German legal material in the English public libraries; the deficiency which was then true of England is still true here ; so much so, that a gentleman familiar with the state of the law in Germany was recently compelled to make the condition of a paper on German legal bibliography a visit to the law libraries of Germany. The late treatise by Messrs. Tompkins and Jencken on Modern Roman Law has done something toward accurately familiarizing English readers with the condition of law in Germany, but its scope necessarily limits its usefulness as an authority on the results of codification in Germany. Since Austin's day[3] great progress has been made by the Germans, and his remarks, quoted by Mr. Carter, hardly hold good at the present time. The literature of the Germans upon the subject of codification is very full. The well-known dispute which arose between Savigny on the one side and Thibaut, Gans, Puchta, Rudorf and Thaden on the other, when it was proposed to codify the entire common law of Germany, has afforded to English and American opponents some of their best material ; much of it having filtrated its way into English soil. Yet little accurate information can be afforded by the consideration of the extreme views of either of these parties ; both views are now conceded to contain elements of profound truth and of profound error. Savigny's party was greatly weakened by the secession of Wärnkœnig, his most considerable follower. Now, even the arguments against codification of Savigny,

---

[1] In this suggestion there is no disposition to speak lightly of the thousands of useful books, repositories of much industry and reflection, which load the shelves of the law libraries ; but rather to intimate that it may be that the days of their usefulness is over, when, as Emerson said, "men must d'e in the first alcove."
[2] For 1873.
[3] He wrote about a half-century since.

himself, are, by reason of his transcendental conception of law, said to be better fitted to a system of planetary jurisprudence than to that of this sphere. Violent as this witticism is, it must be conceded that the very obscurity in which Savigny enveloped his arguments has been a successful hindrance to complete codification in Germany, although, at last, the spell of his mighty name has, by the persistent refutations of his opponents, been broken.

The extraordinary confusion of the law of Prussia in Frederick the Great's day—for until 1848 a single commercial bill would sometimes fall under half-a-dozen rules of law within a comparatively small circuit—gave that philosophically inclined monarch a sufficient motive for amending the form of the law. It cannot be admitted by the friends of law reform that even that sovereign's motive for codification was dynastic, although what his motive was is inconsequential: But they cannot believe that any dynast in his senses would tie down the judges of his own creation to philosophic laws arranged in a code and thus put it out of his power to dictate judicial decisions in some concealed fashion. That Frederick the Great happened to give the first regular impulse to codification in Germany must be admitted, just as it must be admitted that he met with disheartening opposition from the unphilosophic lawyer-class of the Prussia of that day. Under his successor, Frederick William II., the "*Landrecht*," a complete codification of the common law of the whole Kingdom, was promulgated, leaving in force, however, the *ius particulare* of the various provinces. In other German-speaking States codification has ensued: Notably, the Austrian *Gezetsbuch* in 1811 and the Saxon *Gezetsbuch* in 1865. In Baden and the Rhine Provinces, the Code Napoleon was, with scarcely any alteration, adopted. The comparatively recent promulgation for the entire German Empire of the three codes relating to bills and notes, commerce and crimes, as well as the great reforms in the law relating to landed property, induces the party of progress in Germany to hope that the commission now sitting for that purpose will, at no distant day, report a codification of the entire law, thus completing a reform so full of difficulty by reason of the lack of a central influence during the formation of the *ius particulare* of the Provinces and States now composing the German Empire.[1]

Mr. Carter's strictures regarding the results of codification of the private law of Louisiana and California, alone, of his historical parallels, remain to be noticed. It would not be strange if it had been the fact, that codification had failed and failed utterly in Louisiana, a country subjected within less than a hundred years to the political domination of three powers, each possessing a different language and a different jurisprudence. That it has not failed is perceived by the persistent retention of a code, largely foreign in composition and origin, by the now dominant American element in Louisiana. Had this element not perceived the advantage of a lucid and simple form of the law, they would long since, in accordance with the law of nations, have substituted the law of the dominant people; and it is well known that shortly after the annexation of Louisiana such a substitution was proposed. To any one familiar with the disposition of the various races of people in Louisiana, and especially at the metropolis, New Orleans, it will not appear strange that, in the course of the trial of cases not precisely provided for by the code, each element of the population, by its proper agent, appeals to the more familiar or favorable analogies, presented by any recognized system of jurisprudence. It may be true, without affecting the merits of the question of codification at large, that the purely American element, fully represented at the bar, now appeals most frequently to the familiar analogies of the Anglican common law, as it is the substratum of the *lex mercatoria* of Louisiana as well as the ultimate standard of her supreme appellate tribunal. Certainly neither the fact of the present reference, in many Louisiana cases, to the common law of the prevailing Anglo-American type, nor the criticism by a single Louisiana judge of the hardship of the thirty-five definitions contained in the Louisiana code, make out a strong case. The truth is that the people of Louisiana are better satisfied with the law contained in their code

---

1 " Law Reforms in Germany," XVIII., Am. L. Rev., 801, 811.

than with the law which is not in accord with it. The native element in Louisiana, and that is the best element, is a code-respecting people. Many years ago, in the days of Kent and Story who approved it, Gustavus Schmit, a Louisiana lawyer of great erudition, prepared a short history of the jurisprudence of Louisiana; in it is this praise of the then recent French reform: "France, whatever may be thought of the rank which it occupies as an agricultural, commercial and manufacturing country, is unquestionably, so far as it relates to the theory and practice of its civil jurisprudence, in advance of the age, and can afford useful lessons to the rest of the civilized world." It was this spirit, partly reflected from this writer, which enabled the people of Louisiana to arrive at an ultimate codification. Lately, and after a long and adequate trial of its merits, the Code of Louisiana appears to have been re-enacted. Not only has it been re-enacted, but there seems to be no agitation upon the subject and no apparent disposition to substitute that Anglican product which, with some modern improvements, we have the honor to enjoy in this and most other States of the United States.[1]

The recently published testimony of the Californian judges to the practical success of a code of private law in their State, is not impugned by the assertion that the social and political conditions of California are so much more simple than like conditions in this State as to make the feasibility of codification there prove nothing here. The same form of assertion has been made by Professor Amos to the English people in regard to the results of a codification in New York, with the effect of permitting one to think that professional gentlemen who have lived within the sound of "Bow Bells" are not widely different from professional gentlemen who dwell within the sound of Trinity chimes; both have their *idola fori*. The fact undoubtedly is that social and political conditions in California are not widely different from those with us in this State. If at all different, those in California are, as the Federal Supreme Court Reports show, the more complex.

[1] Confirmation of the general view stated may be seen in a late paper entitled, "Civil Law in Louisiana," by Thomas J. Semmes, Esq. (5th Annual Report of the American Bar Association, pp. 212, 250).

The time has gone by when the newer settlement is presumably the more rude: New York started upon the seventeenth century with the accumulated product of European civilization, just as California started upon the nineteenth century with all American civilization behind her. Social conditions which the law recognizes are not now materially simpler here than in England, nor those in California, materially simpler than those here. The modern basis of law is largely contractual everywhere, just as modern society everywhere is now free from those feudal restraints upon *status* that once complicated government by means of the various *imperia in imperio* which the general government was forced to recognize in legal administration. In other words, the mercantile and manufacturing worlds of England and America are not now essentially different; what is law for one is very properly law for the other. That which in England differs from America, relates to the privileged class of the former, and is a remnant of feudalism. This difference is unquestionably growing less, so that some advanced lawyers are already dreaming of a universal codification of the laws of immovable property. It is not necessary to concede the feasibility of such a scheme in order to maintain that there is nothing so complex in the laws of property in New York—and we have no law of a particular *status*—as to cause the Californian code to be a solecism here. If a code of private law works well in California, where everything is commercial and contractual, it will, with some modifications, work well here, where everything is also commercial and contractual, and certainly not feudal, even the manorial tenures which once prevailed in some of the river counties having been wholly obliterated.

At this point a phenomenon, not unnoticed by students of institutions, may be emphasized—the tendency of Americans to adhere to European legal institutions. There is scarcely a dilapidated English law which, when well worn out there, has not found its way here, and sometimes a congenial abode. Sir Edward Sugden (Lord St. Leonards) wondered that Americans could deliberately take up with all the mysterious involutions of the English law of powers, an entirely artificial system invented to unloose the fetters upon the alienation of English real property. Let us only hope that a servile habit of imitation which this betokens, will not restore to us that flagrant antinomy of law and equity, or special pleading, or the miserable subterfuge of the common law concerning consideration and seals, or lastly that bewitching scholasticism, the *scintilla juris*. What Americans want is a rational system of jurisprudence, thought out by themselves, possessing fixed bases, and having its controversial tendency toward principles and ethic, and not to precedents alone. The beginning of this improvement will relate to the form of its *bases*, which is the real subject of this paper.

Having now completed a hurried survey of the States which have had recourse to codification as a means of bettering the condition of their organic law, we may next glance at the theories of codification prevailing in England and America. The nature of the dispute as to the merits or demerits of expressing laws in formulæ, is not new. Students of philosophy will recognize a phase of this very discussion in the distinction which they draw between Plato and Aristotle. Aristotle's aim was to reduce philosophy to science. Plato thought truth too many sided to be shackled by mere verbal expressions. The result is well known ; it was by the inexorable logic of Aristotle that men were first enabled to detect with accuracy the true from the false. The party opposed to codification simply adhere to the old position that truth is too many sided to be shackled ; the party of codification to the old position, that certain fundamental propositions of law may be so formulated as to afford great aid to the arrangement and discussion of the propositions not formulated. [1] It is not strange that Mr. Field is unwilling to repeat in detail the answers long ago conceded to meet the very objections now put forward by the adherents of the historical school of law. It must also be remembered, in this connection, that these answers are already existent in the literature of codification which is extremely complete.

In England the question of codification has for some reason become confused with the discussion concerning the merits of

[1] " Now it is the business of logic to codify, upon abstract principles, the rules of scientific investigations." * * * I Fiske's Cosmic Philosophy, p. 239.

consolidation, revision or other substitutional escape from complications in which their wide-spread empire helps to involve them. The scientific faction of the English bar would, in the main, seem to adhere to a very highly scientific plan of codification. Recognizing that positive laws are concerned either with rights or with duties they are engaged in a discussion as to whether rights or duties afford the best basis for a successful codification—a question about which the practical codifiers of the world have wasted very little breath. • Prof Holland of Oxford, in some respects the most distinguished scientific jurist now living, has but lately succeeded in squaring the circle of the jurisprudents by a distribution of the entire subject-matter of jurisprudence on the basis of rights, a problem Austin notably failed to solve. It ought, at this juncture, to be noted that Professor Holland has disclaimed that his system of jurisprudence was ever intended as a basis of English codification.[1] Other persons, however, less discriminating than Professor Holland, and imbued with the classifications of Austin, Mill, or some other founder of a system, would make these classifications the basis of English codification without regard to the needs of those lawyers who must always practice their profession as an art rather than as a science. The supreme motive in codification—to subject a body of law to a form which best fits it to the concrete purposes of technical law —is thus lost sight of at the outset.[2]

The practical work of codification has always been performed by practical lawyers, those familiar with the needs of practical lawyers. They have generally been men with a scientific bent, but above all possessed of some knowledge of the science of legislation upon which successful codification most depends.[3] By this

[1] In a preface to his Treatise on Jurisp. intended to answer Mr. Tilley's critique, in the London Law Magazine and Review.

[2] Mr. Mill says : " The proper arrangements, for example, of a code of laws depends on the same scientific conditions as the classifications in natural history," and he also says that a scientific code could scarcely have been constructed before the days of the naturalist. Linnæus —(Mill's System of Logic, sixth edition, vol. II., p. 288.) But what practical lawyer can assent to such a theoretical view of codification as this ?

[3] It is so apposite, that the following passage is here quoted : " Il y a une science pour les législateurs, comme il y en a une pour les magistrats ; et l'une ne resemble pas à l'autre. La science du législateur consiste à trouver dans chaque matière, les principes les plus favorables au bien commun ; la science du magistrat est de mettre ces principes en action. de les ramifier, de les étendre par une application sage et raisonée, aux hypothèses privées ; d'etudier l'esprit de la loi quand la lettre tue : "
Motifs, Edit. Poncelet, Discours Préliminaire du premier projet de Code Civil.
History also teaches that in the Greek states, at a very early epoch, the functions of preparing laws were committed to specially trained draughtsmen, νομοθέται. Ordinary training was not deemed adequate.

assertion it is not intended to ignore the great contributions which the scientific and speculative writers have rendered to the cause of codification. It is for example easy to misconceive Bentham's position in this connection and to describe him as an impracticable theorist or enthusiast, for in some respects his convictions induced him to overlook the elements of stability in human affairs. Bentham was great, not as a constructor of codes, but as a scientific legislator. He was the greatest master of the science of legislation who has yet lived ; a *fons philosophiæ* from which all men derive something : " Pillaged by all the world yet always rich," Talleyrand is reported to have said of him. He was barely a lawyer, except nominally or by profession, and yet nearly every legislative reform which he projected has been adopted by the State and its wisdom ultimately acquiesced in by all practical lawyers. An enemy of feudalism and of formalism of all kinds, Bentham is to-day justly regarded as one of the benefactors of the human race. It is not strange that some common lawyers are found to complain of Bentham for he did much to break up the power of the sect which for some centuries claimed to be the exclusive repository of the common law.

As it is easy to misconceive Bentham's relation to codification, so it is easy to misconceive the position of Austin and other legal writers. Austin is *facile princeps* of the English analytical jurists; but his personal relations to codification are insignificant. Possessed of a keen logical faculty, Austin analyzed the elements of jurisprudence with a thoroughness which positively precludes the chance of the reader's misapprehending him. Since his death his teachings have had a powerful influence upon legal thought both in England and America, but his contributions to codification proper are comparatively as nothing, consisting of a few posthumous fragments of a tentative character. In regard to Professor Amos, Mr. Carter's " free lance," it should only be said, as he is still living, either in Australia, Egypt, or England, that he has seen fit to indulge in criticism of all foreign codification, palliating it, in the case of New York, with the pleasing condescension that such a crudity as the Field Civil Code may be well adapted to the crude condition of affairs in this State. This criticism justifies the remark that there is nothing in Professor

Amos' position, which entitles his censure to be regarded as final by Americans ; a voluminous and highly respectable, though not very original,[1] writer, he is but a faint reflection of the masters of jurisprudence whose names have been mentioned. Professor Amos has published, among other things, his own scheme for a code which, though curious as a professorial emanation only— the professorial bent being usually didactic rather than constructive—is not remarkable.[2] In the region of practical codification of the laws of England and her colonial offshoots, of all men past or present, stand preëminent, two American gentlemen, Field and Livingston,[3] and entitled to be mentioned after them are Macaulay, who drafted the Indian Penal Code, Sir James Stephen, who drew the Indian Evidence Act, Sir John Romilly, Mr. Justice Willes, Sir Edward Ryan, and several others whose labors, in some form, have taken practical direction. In the latter list, no doubt, should be comprised Mr. Derbigny and Mr. Moreau Lislet of Louisiana, as well as Duer, Spencer, Butler and Wheaton, the draughtsmen of the New York Revised Statutes, one of the best and most influential pieces of legislation extant, whether we have regard to the reforms it instituted in the common law of real property, or to the general character of the revision.

By a brief examination of extant codes we may perceive not only that the best pieces of modern codification have emanated from practical lawyers, but also that they have not been framed in strict accord with the notions of the speculative writers on codification. The Civil Code of New York, like the Code Napoléon and the Code Frédéric, follows the order of Justinian's Institutes and treats successively of the law of persons, of property and of obligations. Now it is well known that the speculative writers do not approve of the arrangement of any of these codes, for they find in them a lack of logical principles of division, or classification. But the answer to this criticism is that the classes to

---

[1] The Athenæum, an English periodical, sums it all up in an equivocal but discriminating notice of Prof. Amos' work on the "Science of Politics," as follows : "Professor Amos has collected a great many observations and offered a great many opinions, some of which are original, and some of which are valuable." v. Fly leaf, Amos' Rom. Civ. Law

[2] It must, however, be admitted that Professor Amos has the courage of his convictions and that he is in many departments a most pleasing and instructive writer on jurisprudence. It is fair to Professor Amos' qualification as a critic to add that he has lately, in answer to an inquiry of one of Mr. Field's opponents, expressed himself as having entirely changed his former opinion of Mr. Field's codes.

[3] Livingston and his colleagues are enumerated because their labors included a consideration of parts of the English common law.

whom codification is most useful would not appreciate a purely logical principle of dichotomy; they require the rougher and the more practical divisions with which they are, at a glance, familiar. In respect of its arrangement, there has been no criticism of the New York Civil Code, except from such theoretical writers as Amos. At least the anti-code element in the bar societies of New York has made none up to the present time.

The truth of Mr. Carter's most sweeping proposition, now urged against the Civil Code of New York, that all codification is unscientific in theory, depends much on what is meant by scientific. Science is most commonly referable to a body of knowledge arranged in an orderly manner. To be at all relevant to the pending measure, then, this proposition can only mean that in its present state the common law is better arranged than in any code, or else, that any statutory arrangement is unphilosophic. In order to discuss even so plain a proposition, it is necessary to be rid of ambiguous terms and, therefore, to decide in which of its conflicting meanings the term 'common law,' as it is of extended significance, is intended to be used. It has been said that the best way to define 'common law' is by the things to which it is opposed: (1) as contrasted with statute law; (2) with equity; (3) with the law founded on the civil law, with the exclusively local, or military, law. As contrasted with all these things, it is the residuum of a nation's law. There is still another definition quite opposed to the former, or rather inclusive of the very things contrasted in the first definition.[1] In this latter or secondary meaning, the common law becomes the designation of the entire jurisprudence of England, or of any one of its colonial offshoots. Mr. Carter uses this term indifferently, and it is therefore necessary to observe closely in which sense he means it, for the common law of England, in the larger sense of the term, is in a faint degree only identical with the common law of New York.

In the original colonies of England, the common law contains, independently of its mere arrangement, an element of great uncertainty, which it is thought codification will entirely

---

[1] See generally Hale's Hist'y Com. Law, pp. 52-54.

obliterate. The common law of New York, for example, owing
to the colonial conditions under which English law was introduced here, is based upon an illogical hypothesis, most
damaging to its certainty and to legal administration. The
hypothesis in question is that the common law of New York is
fundamentally identical with the common law of England in the
last century, in so far only as this latter is suited to colonial conditions. Now, how far the English law of the eighteenth century
is[1] suited to colonial conditions is one of the most perplexing
problems with which the American judicatories have to deal.[2] It
is not strange that such should be the fact, if we consider the
embarrassment of introducing a body of law made exclusively for
one country into another, far distant and originally not
intended to be included within its operation. Every one knows
of the interest which originally attached to Buckle's attempt to
demonstrate that civilization was the product of climate and
locality, and realizes now that the failure of the demonstration
was inevitable from the vast scope of the proposition. Yet few
will deny that jurisprudence, a component of civilization, is to
some extent a local product, and that its introduction elsewhere,
than in the land of its origin, is full of embarrassment. In order
to make more apparent what is meant by the assertion, that the
common law of New York is founded upon an illogical hypothesis, some further digression must be condoned. About the time
that law of English original was being first introduced by the
English government in countries out of England, the English
institutional writers and, for that matter, many English judges,
frequently resorted to figurative explanations of legal phenomena.
The common law, like the Roman *ius civile*, was made for men
in a certain *status* only and the embarrassment of accounting for
the application of the common law in the English dependencies,
taxed greatly the English judges' ingenuity. With one accord
they finally agreed that the English common law was
in force in the crown possessions "*extra 4 (quatuor) mare*,"
as the possessions in question were quaintly described,

---

[1] It is spoken of in the present tense, because by a curious juridical fiction the fact is being
determined now retrospectively.

[2] Meyers v. Gemmel, 10 Barb. 541.

because it was the "birth-right of English subjects everywhere."
Now it needs no examination to detect that this assertion is purely
figurative. Sometimes the institutional writers went farther into
detail when the English common law was described as introduced
into uninhabited countries, discovered and planted by English
subjects, upon the "birth-right" theory, but into countries conquered by Englishmen by express legislation only.[1] The fact is
this contrast is unsound; law of English original could be introduced into any countries out of England only by express legislation of some sort, and the distinction denoted by Blackstone is
pure fiction. Until new countries are subjected to constituted
authority, the inhabitants are subject to the law of nature only,
and that was the doctrine of the earlier English cases.[2] After a
government is once established the constituted authority promul-
gates laws; and in the case of the English colonies, laws of
English original. Sometimes the legislative machinery has been
and, doubtless, now is concealed in the crown-governor's commission, or in his instructions, but it is always present somewhere.
The institutional writers in order to account for the unfamiliar
limitation usually contained in the colonial constitutions—that the
law of English original should be in force in the new countries
only in so far as suited to the new conditions—proceeded to
amplify their theory accordingly. They chose to regard the
common law as "carried" by the colonists, but only so much of
it as was needed. Yet no one will now pretend that any particular colonist carried any particular law, so that a little reflection
enables us to detect that the commonly received account of the
mode in which English laws were introduced here is figurative.[3]

The result of this early theorizing upon the American colonial
law has not been conducive to certainty in later legal administration and in New York, where we have the largest body of substantive law, it has been most unfavorable. Justice Story, while
not stopping to question the received account of the mode in

[1] Bla. Com., 108.
[2] Dutton v. Howell, Shower's Parl. Cas., p. 31, temp. Car., 11.
[3] In a series of a, no doubt, too desultory observations on New York jurisprudence published
in the Albany Law Journal (Vols. 19-20) the writer of this paper first directed critical attention
to the invalidity of the Blackstonian theory of *extra territorial* common law. He is pleased
to observe that since then Dr. Wharton has given greater emphasis to the discussion, though
from other and often opposite points of view. (See Wharton's Commentaries on American
Law, pp. 48, 102, 103.)

which English law was established here, pronounces the theory
" most perplexing," because of the element of uncertainty, as to
what part of the English common law was in fact in force here.
He adds," It is not easy to settle what parts of the English law
are or are not in force here until either by usage or judicial
determination they have been recognized as of absolute force." [1]
Thus it may be seen that upon any theory the very basis of the
common law of New York is, because of the particular qualification with which its introduction was originally burdened, a much
more uncertain quantity than that of England. But as if New
York was intended to be devoted to the fury of the infernal gods
who preside over its legal institutions, still another hypothesis
comes in at the basis of its particular common law: The judicature of New York has long proceeded to determine what part of
the English jurisprudence was in force here upon the theories,
contrasted by the early institutional writers, that in conquered
provinces the English law was imposed only by legislation,
whereas in newly discovered countries it was transported by the
colonists as their "birth-right." Now whether New York is, for
the purpose of practically applying this introduction theory, to be
regarded as having been acquired by the English by conquest,
or by discovery and *iure occupationis*, under the Romanized law
of nations, the New York judges have been somewhat puzzled to
determine, though giving the preference to the latter view, which,
by the way, is exactly opposed to the historical fact. [2] New York
was in reality conquered by the English from the Dutch, but by
reason of the extraordinary breach of the law of nations which
Charles II. committed when he permitted the Duke of York to make
war with the colony of a power with which England was at peace,
the English claimed New York retrospectively, or before they
had taken it, and as having belonged to them originally by discovery and prior occupancy. Curiously enough this old historical
dispute now lurks at the bottom of our common law and two
centuries later [3] puts suitors to many an unnecessary bill of costs.
It is only necessary to point out further, that not only is the

---

[1] 1 Story on Const., p. 100.
[2] 4 Pai. Ch. 198 ; 3 Barb. Ch. 123 ; 30 Barb. 14 ; 35 N. Y. 458 ; 46 id. 141 : 10 Barb. 544; but see *contra*, 15 Johns. 93 : 5 Wend. 436 ; 6 Hill, 177 ; 15 Johns. 115 ; 37 N. Y. 233 ; 24 Wend. 623-24.
Dunham v. Williams, 37 N. Y. 251, reversing *S. C.*, 36 Barb. 136.

common law of New York subject to the two local hypotheses outlined, but it is involved in an additional one, common to all the original American colonies and provinces : Blackstone in giving a concrete instance of the application of his theory of the common-law introduction into crown dependencies, cited the American colonies as examples of countries acquired by conquest, and added that there consequently the common law of England was set in force by express legislation.[1] Later in the history of American jurisprudence, when it became necessary to account for a law of English original, which was wanted for immediate application, but the chain of title to which was obscure, the Supreme Court of the United States partially rejected Blackstone's theory ; and Chief Justice Marshall most solemnly decided that Blackstone was partly mistaken ; that America was not conquered from the Indians, because the Indians had no national existence to conquer ; and, consequently, that the common law of England was to be regarded as in force here upon the theory that the American colonies were discovered countries and not conquered provinces.[2]

Such, then, are only some of the mischiefs in the administration of a law, the very existence of which is postulated of fictions. Had public attention been directed to an analysis of laws in general, such a monstrous system of judicial riddles would perhaps never have been incorporated in the new State Constitution which re-adopts the common law of the former colony —a commodity the colonists could never determine, and consequently always complained of after the repeal of the " Duke's Lawes," the first code of New York.[3] As a specific instance of the mischiefs occasioned by the uncertainty as to what is, or is not, the common law of New York, the case of Meyers v. Gemmel[4] affords fair illustration. Now codification must ultimately cure all such doubts and uncertainties as are peculiarly referable to the theories just noticed and substitute therefor a private law of American origin, not dependent for its existence

---

[1] 1 Bla. Com. 108.
[2] 8 Wheaton, 573 ; 16 Peters, 404.
[3] This code was a very complete body of private law, and had it not been for the Dutch element in New York it would have been an entirely satisfactory basis for New York jurisprudence. It was enacted in A. D. 1664, and re-promulgated in 1674.
[4] 10 Barb., 541.

on some curious, mediæval utterance, expounded and amplified by the English institutional writers into a theory at variance with fact. In any aspect of the matter it may well be doubted whether a common law predicated of such a double uncertainty can be said to be fundamentally scientific as Mr. Carter has seen fit to suppose it is.

The present disposition of the common law of New York in reports of adjudications, is not entitled to be regarded as more scientific than it would be if arranged in a code. Doubtless, when the number of reported cases is comparatively small no arrangement in lucid order is necessary to the lawyer-class; each trained person being able to supply the deficiency for himself. It is only when the state of the law becomes so diffuse and contradictory as to defy all private attempts at classification that compendiums and abridgments become necessary to lawyers. Now the difference between compendiums and codes is only one of degree. A digest is an arrangement of legal propositions, in alphabetical order, without authority, while a code is a logical, authoritative, statutory arrangement. Professor Holland calls a digest, an "imperfectly developed code," and states, "that as compared with unsystematic law they stand very much in the same position." It is unnecessary to insist upon this analogy further than to say, that it is scientific support for a favorite assertion of Mr. Field's. The disposition of the common law in digests is open to the objection that although it lessens the labor of the investigator it leaves the distribution of the law in the reports open to its peculiar objections. Strictly speaking the common law of New York begins with the Year-books and it ends only with the Weekly Digest. But a distribution of any body of law in thousands of volumes is certainly open to grave objections. In the first place, the reports are most often contradictory and confusing, and in the next place they are frequently made to prove more or less according to the inductive skill of the contender—a process operating very harshly upon a client whose case is in the hands of a defective, or careless legal logician. Before a court of moderate capacity, a

4

lawyer of superior intellect, or industry, will often so arrange the numerous authorities as to entirely obscure for the time being all kind of right disposition in the court; thus, oftentimes, only after an appeal does the meritorious suitor succeed in divesting his case of the clever web of his adversary. Another great objection to case-law is that the vast agglomeration of decisions tends to make the law one of precedent and not one of principle; judges and lawyers are so overwhelmed and confounded by the array of authority that in desperation they shield themselves behind some ill-considered precedent without regard to substantial justice in the given case. But the main defect, after all, in the present disposition of the common law, is its repressive tendency; it is not conducive to liberal views concerning the entire scheme of the law, and it fails to convey the relation which isolated groups of laws bear to the entire body of laws. This is a great defect, for just as few specialists are, from their too concentrated habit, wholly safe advisers, so few accurate deductions may be made from cases relating wholly to one set of principles. The reasons in support of the proposition that a code is the more scientific arrangement of any body of law, might be amplified indefinitely, but if enough has been said to induce the so-disposed to examine for themselves the better authorities on this question, this paper will have accomplished its mission.

One of the more common charges against codification, repeated by Mr. Carter, is, in substance, that it has a tendency to promote, what the scientific writers term logomachy or a war about words, and to the subversion of legal discussion about principles. If the common law were now a simple, well-arranged and compendious body of law, this comparison might contain an element of truth, but in the present dispersed, confused and contradictory state of the reports, augmented by the habitual citation of cases of foreign original—necessary by reason of the fiction that the common law of one State is responsive to all cases—it is unsound. The common law cannot, in its present condition, be assumed to be even relatively a law of principles. Its most elementary principles are so impugned and confused by contradictory and illy-arranged reports as to make all legal discussion a war about precedents, with the result of entrapping the less diligent case-reader. But assuming for argument only, the truth of the assertion, that the common law is a body of principles and not words, though it is most difficult to conceive of principles disembarrassed of words, for practical purposes a body of law should be more concrete. The process of extracting principles, from adjudications, is a very laborious one, requiring the highest order of mental effort. In the hands of the unskilful this process is nearly always fallacious, inflicting unnecessary penalties on the suitor and provoking much unjust litigation. No doubt a few skilful men of logical habit, whose tastes incline to polemics, are not displeased with the weapons which afford them such great opportunities for forensic triumph. They are able to possess themselves of a great number of leading principles accurately deduced from the cases, and to feel that they have a firm grasp of them, without reference to a code. But the majority of the legal fraternity—an exceedingly necessary though perhaps less conspicuous element—have no such satisfaction, and it is to this last class that a code is a blessing in the times of doubt and uncertainty.

Another form of the same accusation, which is the subject of the preceding paragraph, is contained in Mr. Carter's assertion that the common law of New York is at present a law of principles, whereas the Civil Code will be a law of language, with all the imperfections which relate to language. Long ago, Mr. F. Vaughan Hawkins returned a complete answer to a precisely similar assertion then made by Mr. Best, the well-known law-writer, and it would seem proper that their able discussion should have either closed this branch of the controversy or have been recognized as the basis of a new departure. Mr. Hawkins pointed out that this objection to codes failed to note the difference between the earlier and later stages of case-law: When case-law becomes elaborated to a high degree of detail, the function of the judge becomes more and more circumscribed, until at last it ceases altogether to be so much the application of principles as a law of precedents. The objections to a law of precedents are their protean character, their present bulky and dispersed disposition, and that they may be able to prove more or less according to the skill of the advocate, with but little chance of a court's immediately detecting elaborately constructed fallacies. Add to Mr. Hawkins' answer, that a law of principles must become expressed in words in order to be practically applied, and the superiority of case-law vanishes before the claims of a well-expressed code.[1]

Enough has been said to enable the unbiassed reader to gather at least that those in favor of codification differ with the conclusions of their opponents, that codification of the common law will introduce into the law either great error, uncertainty, or any other evil prophesied. Nor will codification arrest the spontaneous development of the common law. All writers on codification agree that the development of new law beyond and in addition to that expressed in a code is inevitable, and that to deal with the new case-law summarily some permanent machinery is necessary. In 1829, the revisers of the statutes of New York attempted to cope with this very problem, in so far as it was related to their own revision, but nobody has ever heeded their suggestions. What this permanent machinery is to be, is one of the problems in England of to-day, but it is one with which this State need have no concern, for the future alone can deal with it. Any attempt to solve it, must, it is thought, fail because of the inability of a legislature to allow for unforeseen political and social variations of considerable magnitude. Entirely new regions for legislation will be discovered and give rise to new classifications which no code of to-day can properly contemplate incorporating in any systematic manner. The limits of codification are the present and the known, not the future and the unknown. Mr. Field has always, in this respect, rejected the notions of his scientific allies, thereby giving other evidence of the eminently practical direction of his labors.[2] If the opposition of Savigny and other writers who are

---

[1] Mr. Carter approves of Mr. Justice Talfourd's criticism of statute law as exemplified by the enormous mass of litigation turning on the Statute of Frauds, without noticing the unfairness of drawing into comparison a statute which almost to a greater degree than any known statute, enters into the common affairs of men. The wonder is that the Statute of Frauds is so seldom drawn into controversy, as almost every contract, excepting the most petty, are affected by it. This statute certainly has been a deterrent of litigation, and its provisions have been only collaterally involved when its construction has been invoked, the cause of action having arisen first.

[2] Mr. Field has upon several occasions expressed his disapproval of another favorite theory of some scientific legislators, that illustrations serve to vivify the text of a statute. There can be no doubt that concrete instances by way of illustration often exclude cases which rationally fail within the spirit of the statute. When a statute is enacted its working operation should be left to the judicature and not controlled by the prevision of its draughtsman.

opposed to codification has accomplished little, it has at least accomplished this, the concession from practical legislators that they cannot pretend to cope with the codification or the redaction of laws not yet in being.

It may be pertinently asked, if codification neither destroys the plethora of law nor remedies the process of evolving new case-law, what can be claimed for it? No doubt much is claimed for it that will never be realized, for some evils are incidental to human administrations of justice which is ideally a Divine institution. But this may safely be claimed for codification: It will tend to certainty in legal administration; it will enable us to remove the enormities of the case-law; it will render the framework of the law more accessible to the unlearned, and, mainly, it will afford more exact bases for forensic discussion. It will also introduce simpler methods of logic instead of the present dispersed and ambiguous premises, covered with the scholia of the treatise-writers and buried in the text of centuries, involving complex or hypothetical syllogism in almost every closely contested case. Another merit may be and is claimed for codification—that it will ultimately necessitate a higher type of legislative activity. When each amendment or addition to law must have precise reference to a skilfully drawn act disposing the entire body of law, the necessity of a permanent corps of technically educated parliamentary draughtsmen will be felt by a sound commercial community and being felt will be forthcoming.[1] And, meanwhile, as property, and not procedure, is affected by the Civil Code, debased legislation will be arrested, as in the case of the original Revised Statutes, which was a code much more radical in character than was ever authorized by the act naming its revisers. The articles of the Revised Statutes relating to Powers and Uses and Trusts have been singularly free from legislative interference, because of the great danger to property which it was perceived lurked in each amendment. To such an extent has this policy of non-interference been the case that the courts have, in at least one instance, been compelled to reform what some have thought the

---

[1] Public attention is already directed to this subject. (See an admirable paper by Simon Sterne, Esq., Counsellor at Law, before the American Bar Association, 30 Alb. Law Journ., p. 223.)

legislature alone should have reformed—the article on Powers, in so far as it was negatively concerned with limitations of personal property.[1]

There is an indirect argument, often repeated against the adoption of the Civil Code, to the effect that the reforms of procedure introduced by the Code upon that subject, have not simplified procedure but have been provocative of much litigation upon insignificant points of practice. The true and complete answer to this negative argument would be a very long one, much of it of an undesirable nature. But there is a ready answer which may be briefly outlined: The details of the Code of Procedure were trivial compared with the several great reforms which it instituted. The trouble has been with its working details which were rendered unsymmetrical, to some degree, at the outset, by unfortunate local hostility to a very beautiful and comprehensive draft. The great merits of the first Practice Code are that it destroyed the flagrant antinomy of law and equity and that since its adoption there has been no instance of a suitor's being turned out of a court unredressed, simply because his charges, if sound, were inartificially expressed, or his prayer for relief, if he were entitled to any relief whatever, improperly stated. A faithful examination of the politico-juridical questions connected with the original Practice Code will some day demonstrate that the apparent faults which later invested it, are not attributable to Mr. Field. As to the conceded reforms which the Practice Code instituted, they have now been adopted by nearly all English-speaking States, and it is but common justice to Mr. Field to admit that he has been most largely their author, and that in consequence elsewhere, if not here, he is regarded as the most influential living law-reformer. Praise which long ago was conceded to him by foreigners, is not gracefully withheld from him by his own countrymen and profession.

The Code of Procedure, enacted in 1848, was, taking all things into consideration, a very wonderful piece of legislation, simple, concise and comprehensive. The revolutions it instituted, the extent of which it is difficult now to understand, were

[1] Cutting v. Cutting, 86 N. Y., 522.

wholly, as every one knows, in the laws relative to pleading and procedure. Had crafty, debased and unsystematic legislation refrained from meddling with the primitive Practice Code, there would never have been valid cause for dissatisfaction with those reforms which Mr. Field originally contemplated.[1]   Indeed, to-day, if there were the slightest effort in the right direction, the adjective law of New York, with all the light of experience, might be readily made the best instead of almost the worst in the world.   But as argument is not made up of assertions, it can only be stated that the limits of this paper do not permit that precise array of historical facts which are necessary to prove these particular assertions in detail, because, and because only, strictly speaking, they are irrelevant to the arguments concerning the Civil Code.   It is but necessary to add, in this connection, that the Court of Conciliation, which was originally a very important part of Mr. Field's plan for the reform of procedure, would have materially aided the systematic administration of law, and have greatly cheapened its cost to the State by a diminution of litigation, a result that must have re-acted on the regular procedure.   This part of his plan, however, unfortunately failed of execution.

Isolated English opinion of the New York Civil Code has been imported into local discussion.   This is going a long way for specific authority concerning the merits of an American statute, but the journey having been taken, why is it that the favorable comments have been left behind?   Professor Holland, the acknowledged literary superior of Professor Amos, has, in a very masterly review of all the codes of Christendom, termed Mr. Field's Civil Code "one of the best codes of modern times."   But it is unnecessary to defer to any of the English reviewers, as their opinions cannot be conclusive; the very similarities of their law and ours misleads them as to the extent of the dissimilarities.   While the writings of the new school of English jurisprudence are of great value here, for philosophy has no local habitat, their comments upon American political institutions, and such the Code would be if adopted, are of doubtful value and rarely entitled to be regarded as authority.

---

[1] See, among other things, Judge Cady's editorial, 6 Alb. Law Journal, p. 297.

Ever since Mr. Field wrote his now famous letter to the late Mr. Gulian Ver Planck, mapping out, there and elsewhere, the first practical and comprehensive scheme of reform in the administration of the common law, he has been justly regarded in England by those who have paid most attention to codal legislation and its cognate topics, as one of the most potent, if not the most potent, of all those who, since Bentham, have thrown their shafts at the anachronisms and antiquities in the common law of English-speaking peoples. To treat the first opinion of Amos as the conclusive embodiment of English opinion is to ignore the verdict which their better sentiment has rendered in favor of Mr. Field's work. But if all the critics in England were hostile to Mr. Field, there can be little doubt that his countrymen would ignore them, for no Englishman living has the claim to distinction as a legislator which Mr. Field may assert if he would. It is difficult to conceive why we are asked to defer to a contrary opinion simply because it bears the impression of a respectable English name, unless it is, that because of our former colonial situation, we are always to regard the Temple as the Mecca at which all things legal concentrate. If we are ever to become legally as independent of England as we are politically, and to rid ourselves of the bitter sneers of those who deride our borrowed jurisprudence, it will not be because of any assistance which Mr. Field's attempt will have received from that large and influential part of our metropolitan bar, most attached to the historical school.

Whatever may be the opinion of a few of Mr. Field's opponents, conspicuous in the City of New York, its denunciations of the Civil Code are not shared by persons equally conspicuous in the country at large. In an address lately delivered by Governor Hoadly before the President, Dean and gentlemen of the Yale Law School, it was said : "The experiment of " complete codification has been twelve years on trial in Cali- " fornia. This code is also in force in Dakota. And this trial " has been attended with the same consequences that have resulted " from partial, or Procedure and Penal, codification elsewhere. " If the testimony of Judge Sawyer of the Federal Circuit " Court, Chief Justice Sanderson and other experts can be relied

" on, the experiment is a success. Twice has this great work,
" with which the honored name of David Dudley Field is indis-
" solubly associated, and which will preserve him in everlasting
" remembrance, if not as the Tribonian of this age, at least his
" precursor, been adopted by the General Assembly of New
" York. And when the veto power is no longer used to check
" its progress, and New York has given it a fair trial, not many
" years can elapse before its adoption in substantially the same
" form may be looked for in at least the majority of the States."
Referring to an earlier draft of the same work, the late Judge
Black, an excellent literary authority, styles it 'as comprehensive
as that of Napoleon, and as minute in its details as that of Livingston.' Many similar testimonials could be produced were
they necessary to strengthen the assertion of this paragraph, that
the enemies of the Civil Code are mainly to be found amongst
a few gentlemen denizened in the City of New York and not
elsewhere.

Granting that the Civil Code is a meritorious draft, yet its professional enemies assert also, that it may disturb rights of property,
and no doubt this suggestion is made in good faith : An inquiry
into its soundness requires us to first investigate the source of the
objection, and next its validity. Is this objection a disinterested
plea in behalf of the property of clients, or is it a plea in behalf
of that property which lawyers possess (a small share of the
statistical total) outside of their avocation ? Assuming that it
may be in behalf of both, is the objection itself sound ? The
Code provides that its operation shall not be retroactive, while
the fundamental law provides that no statute shall affect vested
rights. Is not the assumption, then, that the Civil Code will
disturb vested rights a gratuitous one, calculated to work upon
the known timidity of capital ? Or, is the word " disturb " to be
taken in its untechnical meaning of to disarrange without necessarily injuring ?

The plea that the Civil Code may disturb, but not injure capital, requires little consideration ; it is the purely personal argument *ab inconvenienti.* Assuming again, for discussion only, that
this plea may have some shadow of substance, what is it in
reality worth? The friends of codification will unanimously

reply, very little. The possession of capital is not to be confounded with capital itself, nor the inconvenience of the temporary possessors of property with an inconvenience to property itself. To make this distinction plainer recall, that the philosophy of the classical writers terms that collection of rights and obligations which inhere in a man '*universitas iuris*.'[1] If we regard the man apart from his bundle of rights and obligations—this *universitas iuris*—we shall see some resemblance between *universitas iuris* regarded objectively and a corporation or juristic person. The fragile man himself dies, but his *universitas iuris* devolves upon a successor or, successors and endures indefinitely. If again we consider apart those portions of rights and obligations which attach to a particular piece of property we shall see more sharply contrasted the truth of the distinction denoted. Now, the laws which give rise to these particular rights and obligations, the supporters of codification say are sadly misshapen, archaic and oftentimes irrational, let us rearrange these laws in a more simple, modern, and national form. But the agents of capital reply, while you may not injure property, you are sure to annoy its possessor; perhaps, expose him to inconvenience. These, then, are the several assertions sharply contrasted, and the outcome of the whole of them is the plain question—are future generations to be laden with ancestral burdens simply because the temporary possessors of capital augur some inconvenience to their fleeting and ephemeral possessions in any reform in the too diffuse conditions of a jurisprudence passed over the seas to us? The duty of the Legislature, in an amendment of the law, is not to consider the baseless fears of plutocracy, but the advantages to posterity in all time; not the modern Crœsus, but the countless multitudes of men who will fill the waste places of the world when the modern Crœsus is no more heard of and when, like his eponymous hero, and Midas and

---

[1] This term is no more strained, than *persona* or *ius* from which we derive our technical words, person, justice and jurisprudence. *Persona* means primarily a mask and thus served to indicate the rights which masked the man and constituted his juristic self, or individuality. So, the word *ius* just indicates the bond which originally bound men together, thus pointing to the purely artificial or social origin of all laws. These primitive meanings of greatly extended terms show the importance in highly developed societies of well-chiseled or plainly written laws, neatly arranged, so that all men can see for themselves their fundamental rights. When artifice, technicalities, sophistries and over-refinements shall again, as they must, obscure the codes, new redactions will be necessary, but history shows these cycles are farther apart than is often supposed to be the case.

Crassus and all the host of the Claudii, he, too, shall have joined the shades. Wise laws and institutions are made for peoples, not for persons.

That a considerable body of lawyers should persistently adhere to the traditional form of the law, or to the law as they know it, is not strange when we have reference to the bias created by educational methods and by force of habit. Every avenue to legal preferment has so long been through the ancient methods that any change in the venerable system by one in our midst is in some quarters inclined to be resented as an affront; it is fairly regarded as an encroachment upon personal environment. No property is so personal as his law in the abstract is to the lawyer and its would-be-invader is not regarded with favor by those who, consciously or unconsciously, have this feeling to a marked extent. It may be unfair to regard this as an element of the late discussion and yet we must concede that if there is an opposition without sound reason, it is occasioned by bias and by bias only. Another mode of accounting for unreasonable opposition to a change in the form of the law, relates to the state of our juristic literature. This also is inextricably confused with the traditional form of the law. When we reflect how entirely the contributions of most American legal writers are posed upon the antique models, it is not extraordinary that many of their readers' preference should be for the older arrangement of the law. Yet this feeling cannot be admitted to be universal: Americans appreciate original contributions to literature. The Revised Statutes of New York, though impugned by Chancellor Kent, have been extensively followed; the Field Codes, though derided by a few, have been widely adopted[1] and loudly

1 The following table of dates, cut from a New York newspaper some time since, shows the extent to which Mr. Field's draft legislation has contributed to the legislation of the world :
"The first New York Code, the Code of Civil Procedure, went into effect on the first day of July, 1848. It was adopted in Missouri in 1849. In California in 1851. In Kentucky in 1851. In Ohio in 1853. In the four provinces of India between 1853 and 1856. In Iowa in 1855. In Wisconsin in 1856. In Kansas in 1859. In Nevada in 1861. In Dakota in 1862. In Oregon 1862. In Idaho in 1864. In Montana in 1864. In Minnesota in 1866. In Nebraska in 1866. In Arizona in 1865. In Arkansas in 1868. In North Carolina in 1868. In Wyoming in 1869. In Washington Territory in 1869. In South Carolina in 1870. In Utah in 1870. In Connecticut in 1879. In Indiana in 1881. In England and Ireland by the Judicature Act of 1873 ; this Judicature Act has been followed in many of the British colonies. In the Consular Courts of Japan, in Shanghai, in Hong Kong and Singapore, between 1870 and 1874. The Code of Criminal Procedure, though not enacted in New York till 1881, was adopted in California in 1850. In India at the same time with the Code of Civil Procedure. In Kentucky in 1854. In Iowa in 1858. In Kansas in 1859. In Nevada in 1861. In Dakota in 1862. In Oregon in 1864. In Idaho in 1864. In Montana in 1864. In Washington Territory in 1869. In Wyoming in 1869. In Arkansas in

praised for literary and legislative excellence. The discussion
which has succeeded to all these measures only demonstrates,
that there is a limitation to the soundness of the criticism of
those who have grown up under the purely traditional methods
of legal development.[1]

If Mr. Field's Civil Code be regarded in its literary aspect
alone, it is surely entitled to respectful consideration from a
learned profession, for it is the most completely original work
ever produced by an American legal writer, while for accuracy
of technical expression it is unquestionably the equal of any statute yet drawn in the English tongue. Singularly enough, the
best chronicles of Mr. Field's literary labors are found in foreign
periodicals. Whether this is due to oversight on the part of his
neighbors, or to the greater sagacity of the foreign critical writers,
those competent to judge will ultimately determine. That such
should be the case with the Civil Code is doubtless due to its
having received greater critical attention abroad than at home.
It has figured conspicuously in the legislation for India and in
that for many of the Western American States, while it may be
seen reflected in such tentative productions as Pollock's Specimen
Digest of the Law of Partnership. Nowhere can Mr. Field's
share in the extirpation of the former antinomy of law and equity
be denied. The evidence of the conceded facts then fairly
entitles Mr. Field to speak on codification with an authority
which attaches to no other living utterance. But whatever
difference of opinion there may be as to the expediency of adopt-
ing Mr. Field's draft Civil Code, there ought to be none concerning the value of his contributions to American legal literature,
for it is very great; greater, by far, than that of any other
practising lawyer.

It is sometimes thought by conservative men that the slow
progress of the English nation in the direction of codification is

---

[1] In Utah in 1876. In Arizona in 1877. In Wisconsin in 1878. In Nebraska 1881. In Indiana in 1881. In Minnesota in 1883. The Penal Code, though not enacted in New York until 1882, was adopted in Dakota in 1865 and in California in 1872. The Civil Code, not yet enacted in New York, though twice passed by the Legislature, was adopted in Dakota 1866 and in Cali- fornia in 1872, and has been much used in the framing of substantive laws for India. The Political Code, reported for New York but not yet considered, was adopted in California in 1872."

[1] Mr. Field's Penal Code and Code of Criminal Procedure, adopted in New York in 1881, have met with a most triumphant success, notwithstanding the extraordinary opposition which greeted their inception.

the true one, but without reflecting on the greater uncertainty of the common law of this State, noticed in one particular at a preceding page. The mere fact that the English have not arrived at a codification of the *ius privatum* division of their substantive law is due to several causes, none of which apply here. Their failure is by no means equivalent to their confession that such a codification is either unattainable or undesirable. The order of the changes in the adjective law of the two countries shows us that the English are, in this single respect, our legal debtors, and if we choose they may be our debtors in respect of a codification of the substantive law. As long since as 1851 it was publicly stated in England that the leading English lawyers were then greatly in favor of radical change in the form of the law. They still recognize the desirability of the long contemplated change, but their plan has grown with delay, and is now far more radical than any thing ever contemplated here, and consequently more difficult of achievement. They are meditating a reform so extensive in design and so complete in execution as to entirely obliterate all laws not embraced in its provisions. Meanwhile they are devising means for so digesting and arranging the entire body of law as to enable them to make their violent excisions without danger to the institutions[1] they do not wish to utterly destroy. No doubt when this plan of codification is executed, if it ever is, it will be comprehensive; perhaps the most so that the world has yet seen. But whether it will answer practically is another question—successful codes have not been highly artificial. Institutions are of very slow growth, and eradication, such as that proposed in England, is often attended by unforeseen complications which are not incident to more moderate reforms. But should the proposed plan respond to the hopes of the English reformers, there is no proof that it would answer here as well as the moderate measure drafted under Mr. Field's auspices.

England is a power most important materially because of her vast colonial dependencies, and her legal relations to the latter are regarded by them as important. The Temple sends her

---

[1] " *Institutions* " is used here in the wide sense of the political writers as embracing single laws of importance. *v.* Lieber's Civil Gov., p. 300.

emissaries to the colonies, while appeals come up to London from the four quarters of the globe and are decided often, if not generally, by laws not of English origin. English writers have affected to see in this reactionary influence of colonial and Indian law on the common law of England a resemblance to the influence of the *ius naturale* and the *ius gentium* on the Roman *ius civile*, and have come to believe in a code constructed from the principles of general jurisprudence common to all countries—a result which the teachings of their analytical jurists had prepared them, and to which their composite state now strongly inclines them. If the new ecumenical school of jurisprudence can accomplish a code which will answer in India, at Good-Hope, in Australia and in England there are signs indicating that it will not be unwelcome, and meanwhile the Code for England languishes ; committees of law-lords and distinguished barristers fail to agree and like Lord Eldon, after having doubted for twenty years on a case before him,[1] they still doubt on the case before them and disagree. It is poor counsel to Americans to await at this day the result of pending British reforms, for the English have ceased to afford us a parallel. It is an open question with English writers as to whether the English law proper is not in its last stage of development whereas that of America must have just begun. Narrow as the difference is thought to be and is in externals, the real difference between the essentials of English and American jurisprudence is immense, and it would be as wise for us to wait for England before entering upon an era of practical codification of our *ius privatum* as it would be to await the resuscitation of the Indo-European cult which has been jocosely proposed by one active partisan of Mr. Carter's committee.

Several other propositions, uttered by the opponents of codification, require notice in any account of the discussion, notably the mystical one—for mysticism is most dangerous to codification — that law is best fostered or developed by leaving it wholly to a class of experts who, in imperceptible modes, voice " the national standard of justice." This idea of Mr. Carter's is not entirely new ; it is not very far from the theory which underlies many of Sav-

---

[1] Earl of Radnor v. Shafto, 11 Vesey, p. 453.

igny's arguments and at first glance it must be confessed to be captivating, but in reality it is a plea for the lawyers and that law be relegated exclusively to them. It is distinctly opposed to any legislative interference with law. Carried to its legitimate consequence, this mode of legal development means a dominant legal class, such as the jurisconsults of Rome, or the barrister-class in England. In a country where there is practically free-trade at the bar and where the safer tendency is toward that primitive condition when almost any man might be constituted court-agent to suitors, there can be no very consistent development of law outside of the legislature. The theory of democratic States is that an exclusive class of lawyers shaping the destinies of the State by means of a *ius prudentibus compositum*, is not desirable. The opposite theory demands a highly trained, exclusive class, divided into factions whose controversy is the substitute for legislative debate and whose best work demands the mystery and seclusion of counsel's chambers. But we should not forget that the genius of this country, notwithstanding many debased exceptions, has exhibited itself in legislation. Nearly every single distinctively American institution, either in the region of public[1] or of private law, is due to legislation, not to the action of the judicature. Is not then the true American policy to perfect that which is natural rather than to return to the methods of either Roman or Anglican legal development?—the more especially as our native policy is consistent with a more widely spread knowledge of the law, the foreign, with a narrow learning, inevitably tending to sophistries and to over-refinements.

The Civil Code, reported as a legislative bill by Mr. Field, has unfairly, as some persons venture to think, been the subject of adverse criticism—criticism, it must be confessed, occasionally uttered by gentlemen eminent in the practice of the law. But eminence in the practice of the law, it should not be forgotten, does not alone entitle a criticism of codification to be regarded as final, or even as oracular. Codification is a science, a science of the form of the law, possessing a literature of its own, quite apart from ordinary

---

[1] The Constitutions in America are a species of legislation and are supposed to be subject to the ordinary rules of statutes relating to repeal by implication.

juristic literature. An eminent legislator, Sir James Stephen, expressed surprise that a lawyer of undoubted ability as a practitioner was able, in a considerable space of time, to even understand the details of the Criminal Code, his attention never before having been directed to the science of legislation. This surprise indicates, at least, the value Sir James Stephen would place upon the off-hand opinions of eminent practising lawyers. The retort of the so-called practical men to any such suggestion as this is, of course, that the exponents and disciples of codification "undervalue the teachings of experience." This retort may be true in some instances; it is in no degree true of Mr. Field, and is true *sub modo* in any instance. The theoretical codifiers undervalue the teachings of experience, no doubt, but to the same extent only that the empirical practitioners undervalue the teachings of science and philosophy. If the purely legal scientist is too much engrossed with his abstractions to be a wise legislator for the wants of law-men, certainly the purely practical lawyer is too much engrossed with his docket, to apt to gaze at public questions from his office window, to be a safe criterion of the true legislative policy of a State. But the natural opposition between these widely opposed schools of lawyers is not new. We see it fully delineated in Cicero's *De Legibus;* in his sneers at the quibbling trifles of the practical lawyers; in his patronizing query to Atticus, "Would you have *me* put forth little treatises on Servitudes and Party Walls?"[1] In view of Cicero's defined position, it is not strange that those who pride themselves on being practical lawyers, are induced to join in the modern censure of Cicero, and to forget that Cicero's weaknesses — weaknesses never impairing the majesty of his splendid intellect — were external. When Mr. Carter takes his turn at Cicero's technical deficiencies, it only exemplifies how much human nature is alike at different epochs, for if Mr. Carter thinks lightly of Cicero's legal attainments,[2] it is equally true that Cicero thought

<hr/>

[1] *De Legibus;* "ut libellos conficiam de stillicidiorum ac de parietum iure?"
[2] Cicero was a pupil of Scaevola, the founder of scientific juris-prudence, and no doubt mastered the entire gamut of positive law, then in a comparatively narrow compass. This is shown by what Atticus is supposed to say to Cicero, "Nam a primo tempore aetatis iuri studere te memini, quum ipse etiam ad Scaevolam ventitarem, neque unquam mihi visus es ita te ad dicendum dedisse, ut ius civile contemneres."— *De Leg.* I, *cap.* IV. There is abundant evidence to show that Cicero despised the conventionalities which the technical anti-reform lawyers of that day delighted in, and that his position was deliberate.

lightly of the attainments of the practical men who, Mr. Carter intimates, are not now consulted by the "apostles of codification."

This digression permits one to further empasize that the dispute between the historical school of law and the philosophical school of law is the creature of no age or clime. As German discussion relative to codification shows, the true standard of legal progress is midway between practice and theory; a little of both, not too much of either. The mental make-up of many of the practical men who instinctively resist all change in the form of the law and in legal evolution, would have induced them, had they lived at an earlier day, to have resisted every change in the common law which the past two centuries have effected; they would have delighted in the barbarous law-jingle prevailing in England down to the reign of George II., and in that bewitching conceit, that the seizin to feed contingent uses by a *scintilla juris* was *in mare*, *in terrâ, in custodiâ legis*, or anywhere a disordered fancy could imagine it. They would, in short, have maintained the old court of chancery, even though its curious proceedings often absorbed the entire estate protected,[1] for the law to them is the one thing which must not be subjected to change; it is the one old thing never to be improved.[2] History shows, in short, that in no country in the world has codification been greatly promoted by lawyers as a class. There seems to be an indescribable charm in the modes to which they are accustomed, and an abhorrence of change of all kinds. While this conservatism, doubtless, has the merit of adding an element of stability to American institutions,[3] it is sometimes fatal to progress in the right direction. Without intending to even intimate that Mr. Carter's personal objections to codification are open to any such coarse criticism as that just here made, the criticism itself is not without force when applied abstractly to class-bias and tendencies.

---

[1] Phillimore's Dissertation on Jurisp. Intd.

[2] Goethe says (Faust, Part I, f. 4):

" Your laws must be antique to please,
Hereditary, like disease,
Slowly they pass from race to race
And drag themselves from place to place.
Obscure has grown what once was plain,
What was a benefit, a bane.
Alas, that rights we should have none
Save from our fathers, dead and gone! "

[3] De Tocqueville, Democ. In America, *passim*.

5

After open declarations against the utility of any codification of the common law, political expedients have been resorted to in order to defeat the passage of the New York Civil Code. Its enemies have urged such half-measures as the propriety of appointing a committee of eminent specialists, to be competently paid while they lend their additional qualifications to the developing of a *real* code in fractions. If such a committee were appointed it is most doubtful whether it could achieve a code at all equal to the Field Civil Code, either in execution or in utility. Thibaut and all other writers on the science of legislation agree that a good code can be developed only under the auspices of one mastermind. This would be *à fortiori* true of a code wrought by a committee of eminent specialists, each accustomed to magnify the importance of his specialty, even if his concentrated habit had not impaired his opportunities for the study of the larger or cognate subdivisions of positive law. In a republic, the additional difficulty in such a committee would be found in selecting the Papinian[1] of the committee, for it would be a fatal admission to declare, as the Romans did, any citizen *excellentissimo ingenio vir* when in fact we know that in America all are equal in the law. Neither the fact that Mr. Field has been the master-spirit in the construction of the Civil Code of New York, nor the fact that its cost has been trifling to the State, are worthy objections to the codification in question. It is certainly not strange, in a country where the dignity of the State is not supported by the outward condition of its ministers, that the best public work has not been performed by highly paid commissioners. The Revised Statutes cost but a trifling sum, less, indeed, than a late ponderous revision of the municipal ordinances of the City of New York. Certainly its cheapness to the State should furnish no valid argument against the Civil Code reported by Mr. Field.

It is beyond the province of this imperfect essay to attempt to do more than to furnish the answers usually made, by a certain school of thought, to such objections as those so eloquently expressed in Mr. Carter's recent paper against codification. It is not purposed to discuss at large the value of the specific criticism made by several lawyers concerning the details of Mr. Field's

---

[1] Justinian made Papinian controlling when the *juris auctores* disagreed, or were tied.

Code, or further than to attempt to point out that several of the best of these criticisms are not sound. To endeavor to do more than this would be an encroachment on Mr. Field's own prerogative, his able answers to the specific objections to the Civil Code having afforded the best evidence of its intrinsic excellence.

That certain specific criticism of the Civil Code is not sound, is made apparent by a consideration of the late comments by a distinguished lawyer—known to be attached to the historical school—upon the chapter relating to "Servitudes." [1] It is objected, by this unquestionably learned man, that the whole subject of "implied easements" has been omitted from the Civil Code, although since Pyer v. Carter, [2] it has attracted great attention. At the very time that this objection was made, its writer either overlooked, or more likely ignored, the fact that Pyer v. Carter had been expressly overruled, [3] having first occasioned considerable mischief in England and in this country. The same error of reasoning which occasioned "Pyer v. Carter" unquestionably led to Judge Selden's florid and even inaccurate statement of the doctrine of implied easements in Lampman v. Milks, [4] and to a good deal of unnecessary litigation. [5] No worse nuisance could be imposed upon a law of real property than a refined system of implied easements, as every owner of real estate will bear witness. This particular objection is not only evidence, then, of the tendency of even great lawyers to hypercriticise a very meritorious work, but of the danger which attends a growth of law by judicial refinements after a nation has once attained to a luxuriant crop of case-law.

Mr. Carter's own criticism of the article of the Civil Code relative to "General Average," is astute rather than generous. After the York and Antwerp rules had been sanctioned by the Association for the Reform and Codification of the Law of Nations, Mr. Field redrafted this article so as to make it conform

---

1 This objection serves to show that the training of the technical lawyers induces them, in every age, to attach importance to much the same sort of doctrines. Cicero had a horror of the attenuated refinements with which the Roman lawyers delighted to surround "Servitudes." So have all people who think as Cicero thought of technical law, while the opposite school attach great importance to "implied easements," and delight in the involutions of its doctrines.

2 1 H. & N., 916.

3 Suffield v. Brown, 10 Jur. N. S., 111; Crossley v. Lightowler, 15 Week. Rep., 801; Wheeldon v. Burrows, 28 id., 196.

4 21 N. Y., p. 505.

5 Outerbridge v. Phelps, 13 Abb. N. C., 117.

to the recommendation of the association of which he is so distinguished a member.[1] Fully versed with the latest and broadest view of the publicists upon this subject, Mr. Field was enabled to foresee that this branch of the law was of such universal operation and interest that petty local laws must soon disappear. His prognosis has already been fully verified, the Chamber of Commerce of the State of New York having very lately taken action through the Federal Secretary of State with the view of bringing the law of this State into accord with the law of other commercial nations. Should the determined action of the Chamber result, as it eventually must, in success, Mr. Field's Code will consequently need no additional amendment in respect of its provisions relative to General Average.[2] No further comment upon the specific objections to the Civil Code can be necessary in order to induce the unprejudiced to think that there is another side of the Civil Code besides that presented by its enemies.

But conceding that the Civil Code is not perfect, and it may safely be assumed that no perfect code will ever be constructed, yet a poor code is better than no code. Mr. Frederick Pollock has well said "That the principal lesson to be learnt from the French codes is that even a very defective code is far better than none." Such has been Mr. Field's modest plea for his own masterly hand-work. No doubt this will be a very inadequate recommendation to many, but it is nevertheless the verdict of that actual experience, which is asserted to be so potent when invoked on the other side of this code controversy.

The finality of Mr. Carter's admiration of the common law as it is, even conceding to the judiciary establishment a greater

<hr/>

1 Mr. Field lately brought up a plan before the association for subjecting Asiatic States to the Law of Nations.—London Law Mag. and Rev. for 1883-4.

2 Mr. Carter prints a letter from a gentleman whom he terms "an eminent average adjuster." The letter itself is calculated to disturb timid people to whom general average is an occult science. This letter asserts in substance, that the Field Code will throw this highly important branch of law into confusion. Now the duties of pure average adjusters of marine losses are largely clerical, and "General Average" is by no means a structure on which our jurisprudence depends. The English Lloyds, the greatest of underwriters, very recently expressed themselves in open hostility to the whole system of "General average," recommending its total overthrow and abolition. To this short-sighted policy statesmen and jurists do not accede, though they recognize the necessity of a reform which takes its last expression in the York and Antwerp rules. The great dissatisfaction with the extraordinary claims of the average adjusters has also reached the courts, and in Atwood v. Sellar, Lords Cockburn, Bramwell, Baggallay and Thesiger, expressed a very decided opinion about the anomalous authority of the "average adjusters," overturning one of their customs of eighty years' duration. Is it not a fact that one mode of calculating averages rather than another, is not a matter which is going to disturb the foundations of society or even of jurisprudence?—the whole body of average adjusters to the contrary notwithstanding.

power of change than he would think consistent with its functions, is that no statutory change whatever can be for the better.
The difficulty with the present state of the law—and Mr. Carter
admits that there is a difficulty—is, he thinks, only with the
judiciary, and with the decline in the character of legislation.
There may be room for improvement in both the directions thus
indicated, but far too much is laid at the door of the judiciary
which should be placed elsewhere. The judiciary of the State of
New York very fairly represents the bar. Both bench and bar are
the result of traditional methods of legal education, if education
that may be called which has been picked up anywhere and
anyhow. It is said, for instance, by those competent to judge,
that there is not a single institutional treatise on the common
law which is adapted to the purposes of sound legal education.
Certain is it that the antique mode of legal training in vogue
with us, while it is not wholly unsuited to mere practical success
at the bar, is not unlikely to be at the root of that which Mr.
Carter would lay at the door of the judiciary and the legislature.
We should all take our just share of the blame which attaches to
the present condition of things. Few of us can deny that we
would not have profited by having approached jurisprudence in a
more scientific fashion.

The school to which Mr. Field belongs and certainly leads, in
this country, thinks that it perceives the remedy for the acknowledged legal ills, in the reform of the form of the law, in simpler and
more direct legal methods, and in a higher, though still voluntary,
type of legal education. Is not the plan worth trying?

This is an era of legislation, in Europe, in South America
and elsewhere. Not a civilized nation, England not excepted,
but addresses itself seriously to the work of codification, and to
the simplification of traditional legal methods. Here, as elsewhere, codification of the substantive law must come. If it
does not come in the shape of Mr. Field's legislative draft, as
there is no adequate preparation for a better, it will come in a
less meritorious form, but it will come. When it does come, the
merits of Mr. Field's Civil Code will not be denied, for, legal
literature has its own Nemesis who both punishes the ungener-
ous critic and ignores unjust censure of honest effort.

THE END

www.ingramcontent.com/pod-product-compliance
Lightning Source LLC
Chambersburg PA
CBHW030026030726
47499CB00008B/3138